TROUBLE FOLLOWS

MONICA McKAYHAN

TROUBLE FOLLOWS

An INDIGO Novel

TM

TROUBLE FOLLOWS

ISBN-13: 978-0-373-83087-9
ISBN-10: 0-373-83087-4

© 2007 by Monica McKayhan

www.KimaniTRU.com

Printed in U.S.A.

FRESH. CURRENT. AND TRUE TO YOU

Dear Reader,

What you're holding is very special. Something fresh, new and true to your unique experience as a young African-American! We are proud to introduce a new fiction imprint—Kimani TRU. You'll find Kimani TRU speaks to the triumphs, problems and concerns of today's black teens with candor, wit and realism. The stories are told from your perspective and in your own voice, and will spotlight young, emerging literary talent.

Kimani TRU will feature stories that are down-to-earth, yet empowering. Feel like an outsider? Afraid you'll never fit in, find your true love, or have a boyfriend who accepts you for who you really are? Maybe you feel that your life is a disaster and your future is going nowhere? In Kimani TRU novels, discover the emotional issues that young blacks face every day. In one story, a young man struggles to get out of a neighborhood that holds little promise by attending a historically black college. In another, a young woman's life drastically changes when she goes to live with the father she has never known and his middle-class family in the suburbs.

With Kimani TRU, we are committed to providing a strong and unique voice that will appeal to *all* young readers! Our goal is to touch your heart, mind and soul, and give you a literary voice that reflects your creativity and your world.

Spread the word…Kimani TRU. True to you!

Linda Gill
General Manager
KIMANI PRESS

KIMANI PRESS™

For my Granny, Rosa A. Heggie. You are special
in so many ways, and the strongest woman I know.
My life is rich because of you.

Acknowledgments

God is the source of my talent and blessings.

For all the young men and women who told me that *Indigo Summer* was the first book they read from cover to cover. I think you're awesome! To my sons, nieces, nephews and cousins who took me back to being a teenager for the sake of the *Indigo Summer* series. And my family and close friends who keep me grounded.

CHAPTER I

Jade

My head bounced against the leather seat, the headphones of my iPod on my ears, the latest copy of *Vibe* magazine facedown in my lap, and a little bit of drool crept down the side of my mouth. When I felt a little turbulence, I sat straight up, looking around to grasp my surroundings. We were still in the air. Had to be. Because when I peered out of the small porthole window, I saw nothing but white clouds all fluffy and smooth, like huge pillows in the sky.

My mind wandered back to the scene at the airport. My mother was trying to be all hard, but I knew she wanted to cry because I did. This would be the first time in all of my fifteen years that we'd be separated—forever. Or, as she put it, at least until I got my stuff together. She had to feel it. But she just stood there, with that goofy look on her face, holding on to my little sister's hand for dear life, so Mattie wouldn't run off and get lost. She hugged me, but then pulled away quickly, turning her face from me. My mother was never the mushy, kissing-and-hugging type. She hardly ever even told me she loved me. Only in conversation. Like she might say, "Jade, I'm only whipping your behind because I love you." She never just hugged me before bed, like white kids' mamas did, and said, "You know what, Jade? I love you." Never that.

My daddy, on the other hand, was always kissing and hugging my sister and me. He always told us how much he loved us. Every single day he told us. And he listened to us—listened to our thoughts, our ideas. And he didn't fuss nearly as much as my mother did. She was always fussing about something. No wonder my daddy packed his things into a U-Haul and moved away from us. I remember that day like it was yesterday. He'd come home late—really late—again. And Mama was really mad. She started an argument with him and told him that she wanted him to move out. He pleaded with her to change her mind, but her mind was made up. The next thing I knew, he was gone. He moved into an apartment on the other side of town, where Mattie and I only got to visit him every other weekend. Then, as if *that* wasn't enough, Mama decided to up and move us away. Just smack out of the blue, we packed up and moved to my grandmother's house in Jersey.

Just when I was about to experience the time of my life—going to high school for the first time, trying out for the dance team and hanging out with my best friend, Indigo—she took all of that away from me, just like that.

Now, separated from my father and my best friend, I knew for sure that my world had come to an end. But Mama didn't care. She only cared about her own agenda, and making my daddy suffer for making her mad. She didn't care that I hated New Jersey and living with my grandmother who made us go to church three, sometimes four, times a week. She didn't care that I didn't know a single soul at my new high school. She didn't even care that my grades dropped and that I'd lost ten pounds because I stopped eating. And every time I tried to explain it to her, she simply said, "Jade, you just have to give Jersey a chance. You'll meet some new friends soon."

I did meet some new friends, but they weren't Indigo. Indigo and I had history. We had been friends since kindergarten, and that was something that couldn't be replaced by new friendships. And I missed my daddy like crazy. I called him every single night, but it wasn't the same as seeing him—in the flesh—every day. And he missed us, too. I could hear it in his voice. We were the apples of his eye—Mattie and me. He told us so all the time.

I had to do something and get Mama's attention somehow. She wouldn't listen to my pleas, so I put together a plan of action. I started skipping school, stopped turning in my homework assignments and started giving my teachers a hard time. My plan was to get Mama's attention one way or another. Once the teachers started calling, she'd have to take notice after all, and realize how unhappy I was. She would hear my cries when I landed myself into out-of-school suspension. Ten days was the minimum for sassing a teacher, so I went for it.

When Mr. Douglas, the assistant principal, called Mama at work, I was sitting in his office, my arms folded across my chest with my lip poked out as I proclaimed my innocence—even though I knew I was straight-up guilty. I had to play the part just right. Make them all believe I was just a victim of circumstance, at least until my mama packed us up and moved us back to Atlanta. That was my goal—to get my family back together. And it was working, until I got home and felt that thick leather belt against my backside. That wasn't supposed to be a part of the plan. But you can't win every battle during war. There are always casualties, but the war wasn't over yet.

I overheard her talking to my daddy that night on the phone, telling him how I was out of control.

"I don't know what's wrong with Jade," she'd said. "She is getting to be a handful, Ernest. And I can't do this by myself."

The next thing I knew, I was on a plane headed for Atlanta. As much as I missed my daddy and wanted to live with him, my plan was to reunite my whole family, not get sent away like some juvenile delinquent. But here I was, in the window seat on a flight to Atlanta, wondering if my dad's beating would be any worse than the one I got from my mama. I guessed I would soon find out.

My father stood at the top of the escalator at Hartsfield–Jackson Airport, his trench coat opened, a half smile on his face. I could tell he was frustrated. I'd disappointed him. It was written all over his face. What did he think of his little Jade-bug now after reading that five-page letter from my school's principal—the one that spelled out every curse word that I had used and a few that they just threw in there for the heck of it? It was true that teachers made up stuff sometimes, just to make it sound good. My heart pounded as I tried to read Daddy's face, my eyes locked with his. Was it really possible for a father to stop loving his daughter? Surely I wasn't his baby girl anymore, not after my behavior.

"Hi, Daddy," I said, biting my thumbnail and putting on my best innocent voice—the one that had gotten me out of so many whippings in the past. My daddy was a sucker for the innocent voice and the sad eyes that I only used in cases of emergency.

"Jade-bug." Daddy grinned from ear to ear. "How was your flight, baby girl?"

Wow! He called me Jade-bug and baby girl all in one sentence. Guess he still loved me after all.

"My flight was fine. I slept most of the way."

"Good." Daddy grabbed my carry-on gym bag and slung it across his shoulder. "You hungry?"

"Starving," I said, and followed my father toward the baggage claim area.

"Good. I know just the place."

Daddy's SUV pulled into a space at the Varsity, a smile across his face.

"Your favorite place, right?"

"No, Daddy, this is Mattie's favorite place." I

frowned. Had we really been gone that long that he'd forgotten where I liked to eat? "My favorite place is Burger King, remember?"

"Oh yeah, that's right. You like the Whopper, hold the cheese and pickles, cut in half, large Coke mixed with Sprite, and make sure the fries are crispy, right?"

"You remembered." I smiled.

"Yes, I did." Daddy pinched my nose like he used to when I was five. "But we're eating at the Varsity today. Since we're already here and all."

"Cool," I mumbled. "I can always use a good laxative."

I followed Daddy inside and he ordered us cheeseburgers, fries and Cokes.

"Grab some napkins and I'll get us a booth."

I pulled a handful of napkins from the dispenser on the counter, grabbed a couple of straws and found my way toward the booth where I caught Daddy stuffing a handful of my fries into his mouth. He gave me this innocent look as I slid into the booth.

"You been eatin' my fries, Daddy?" I asked.

"Got my own fries, Jade-bug," he said, and then dug into his own. Meanwhile, mine were half-gone.

"It's not cool to eat people's French fries, Daddy," I said while unwrapping my burger. "Not cool at all."

"Well, tell me what's cool because I'm thinking that it's very uncool to sass your teachers like you did the other week." Daddy's face became serious. I was just teasing, not meaning for this to turn into an issue about me. How did we get here from an order of French fries? "What's going on with you, Jade-bug?"

I just went for it.

"Daddy, I hate New Jersey. Didn't want to move there in the first place."

"I know, baby girl, but that's the place that your mother chose for you to live."

"Why didn't you fight it, Daddy? We're your kids, too. You could've sued her or something."

"Barbara wanted to be near her family. I couldn't fault her for that."

"What about what we wanted? We wanted to be near you. You're our family, too." I stuffed a handful of fries into my mouth. "Why did you have to break up in the first place? Everything was just fine."

"Everything wasn't just fine. Your mother and I had been having problems for a long time, Jade."

"Couldn't you go to counseling or something?" I asked, not really expecting an answer, but I was grasping for straws at this point.

"There were a lot of things we could've done, honey, but it's too late for that now."

"It's not too late. You're single. And Mama's single. So get back together. Simple."

"It's not that simple, sweetheart."

"Yes, it is."

"No," he said, and stopped chewing. "It's not."

"Give me one good reason why."

"I've met someone else," he said. I couldn't believe my ears.

"What?"

"Yeah. Her name is Veronica. I can't wait for you to meet her, baby. You're really going to love her."

My heart started pounding at full speed. It was as if time stood still, and my heart was the only thing moving, pounding so fast that my brain could hardly keep up. Did he say that he met someone? Surely I'd heard him wrong.

"What're you talking about? What are you saying?"

"I'm saying that I've met someone and I want you to meet her."

"No," I said. That was all I could think of to say.

My life was falling apart. This was not supposed to be happening. My plan was to get my parents back together, not to have some Veronica home-wrecker person ruin my life. Yeah, I wanted to meet her alright. I had something for her.

My daddy sat across from me at that table, smiling and chewing on that nasty, greasy Varsity burger. I wanted to slap that silly smile off his face!

CHAPTER 2

Indigo

I sat in the computer chair, my backpack on the floor, my shoes kicked off and my feet propped up on his bed. Tapping the eraser from my pencil on the arm of the chair, I studied Marcus as he intently checked my homework assignment for errors. I waited for him to look up from my math book, but he wouldn't. Not until he was finished marking up my paper in red ink, like he was crazy.

"Indi, you gotta redo all of these," he finally said.

"Marcus, I don't understand that stuff. It's foreign to me."

"Well, come here, let me show you." He tapped a place on the bed next to him, signaling for me to join him there.

I plopped down beside him on the bed, glancing over at his television as Beyoncé shook her booty on a video on BET's *106 and Park*.

"Show me what?" I flirted with the boy who had become my boyfriend only thirty-seven days ago, although it felt as if I'd known Marcus all my life. He made me feel so comfortable, so special. He was everything a girl could want in a guy: he was smart, mature, made me feel like a princess and he was *so* fine!

I caressed his face with my French-manicured nail.

"Indi, I'm serious," he said, grabbing my finger and holding it tight. He was so cute when he was serious.

"I am, too." I ignored him as my lips gently brushed his. He didn't kiss back, but he didn't move away either.

"You have a lot of mistakes on your homework, baby." That crease in his forehead let me know that he really wasn't playing with me. "I need you to take your homework more seriously."

Was he for real? He sounded just like my father. Still, my hand began to caress his chest.

"Play now. Work later," I whispered in his ear.

"No," he said, grabbing my wrist firmly. "Work and then play."

"You're no fun," I said and snatched my book and

homework assignment from his lap. I stretched out across his bed, staring at the page that Marcus had marked up in red ink.

"You want me to explain it to you?" he asked, standing, his wife beater hugging every inch of his muscles. His jeans sagged as he picked up a barbell and began pumping weights.

"No, I can figure it out," I lied, as I struggled to understand problems that seemed foreign to me. Math came so easy for Marcus. I pretended to understand because I didn't want him thinking that he had a dummy for a girlfriend.

"It's okay to ask for help, Indi. That's what I'm here for." He continued to pump iron. "It doesn't mean you're dumb or anything. You're dumb if you don't ask for help."

"Okay, okay. Explain it to me." I decided to give up the act.

"Thought you'd never ask." Marcus dropped the weights and plopped down on the bed beside me.

He began to explain math, only my mind began to wander and my eyes followed. I studied the curve of his lips as he spoke. Remembered his kisses and wished his lips were against mine at the moment. My eyes studied the roundness of his shoulders, and then bounced against his chest.

"Are you paying attention, girl?" he asked.

"It's hard to focus when you're wearing that wife beater, Marcus."

"You a trip." He laughed, then grabbed his hoodie that was thrown across the chair and pulled it over his head. "That better?"

"Well," I said thoughtfully, "I was actually hoping you would take the wife beater off."

At that moment, Marcus cocked his head to the side and gave me a strange look. Then he wrapped his arms tightly around me. His lips touched mine as I took in the taste of the peppermint that he'd just popped into his mouth. As his tongue found the roof of my mouth, I wondered if this was the day I would lose my virginity. Marcus hadn't rushed me into anything. Said we should take it slow, and we would only move to the next level when we were both ready. He kept saying that we would both know when the time was right and that we had to be responsible about it.

Marcus was nothing like my last boyfriend, Quincy, who was just the opposite and wanted to rush me into something that I just wasn't ready for. He was the star of the football team and claimed that if I didn't give it up, he would get it from someone else. Well, that's exactly what happened. He found someone who was more willing, and dumped me on Christmas Day, of all days. It was Marcus who had been there to pick up the pieces of my broken heart. He was my guardian angel, my protector, my knight in shining armor.

I was ready.

"Now, back to work," Marcus said, pulling away from my embrace and opening the book again.

I felt magic and saw stars when he kissed me. Hadn't he felt the same magic, seen the same stars?

I frowned at him. When was he going to be ready?

"I gotta go," I said softly.

"Go where?" he asked as I stood, closed my math book and stuffed it into my backpack.

"Home," I said. "Got chores to do."

"What's wrong, Indi?"

"Nothin'." I put my pink-and-white Air Force Ones back on and laced them up. I threw my backpack over my shoulder. "I'll call you later."

"You gon' finish your homework?"

"Yeah, Marcus, I'm gonna finish my homework. I'm not stupid!"

"Nobody said you were stupid, Indi." He gave me a strong hug and kissed my forehead. "Call me when you finish your chores."

"Later, Marcus."

I opened the door to his room, ran down the stairs and out the front door. Since I lived right next door, it was a short trip home. I stepped inside my house and went straight for the kitchen. Mama had cooked smothered pork chops, and I didn't hesitate to drop my backpack in the middle of the kitchen floor, grab a plate from the shelf and load it down with food. I grabbed a seat at the kitchen table and stuffed food into my mouth like there was no tomorrow. Finished an entire plate in less than five minutes flat. Washed it down with a large glass of Kool-Aid. Burped. Rinsed my plate, glass and the rest of the dishes in the sink. Loaded them into the dishwasher and started it. Wiped off the counters and stove, and then grabbed my backpack.

I rushed upstairs, and as I crept past my parents' room, I heard a strange sound coming from behind their door. Sounded like a whimper. Then silence. Then another whimper. I knocked, but didn't wait for anyone to invite me in. I pushed the door open. Mama sat on the edge of the bed, her eyes bloodshot.

"Mama, what's wrong?" I asked as my heart pounded. "Did somebody die?"

"Hey, Indi," she said, standing up and then pretending to busy herself, straightening pillows and stuff. "No. Nobody died. Did Marcus help you with your math?"

"Yes, ma'am," I said, still skeptical about her tears. "Why are you crying?"

"Nothing to worry yourself about, baby. Did you eat dinner?"

"Yes, ma'am."

"Did you clean up the kitchen? Wipe down the counters and stove?"

"Yes, Mama, I did."

"Good, then go on in there and clean up that room of yours, Indi. It looks a mess."

I stood there for a moment, staring at my mother who had been crying about something, but was now pretending there was nothing wrong. What did she take me for?

"Well, go on." She pushed me out of her room and I went, but reluctantly. I would be back for some answers, Carolyn Summer. I needed to know what was wrong.

I slowly made my way to my room, where I dropped my backpack. I rushed into my bathroom, leaned over the toilet and stuck my finger clear down to the back of my throat. The pork chops and mashed potatoes were good, but they were a one-way ticket to obesity. It had been Monique Jones who had carefully brought to my attention the pounds that I'd picked up over the holidays, and that if I wasn't careful, I'd be too fat and out of shape to remain on the dance team. That was not an option.

Only certain girls were lucky enough to make the dance team. They had to endure strenuous tryouts. Some girls were cut from the team, but the girls that remained were the ones who had the most talent. And I was among those few that remained. It was a privilege, and I wouldn't jeopardize that for a few unnecessary pounds.

"The dance team is no place for big girls, Indi," she'd said with a laugh.

The dance team. The team that had been my sole purpose for wanting to go to high school. A team that I'd tried out for at the beginning of the year, successfully making it to the finals. It was one of the most important things I'd ever accomplished in my life. I couldn't risk losing it all because I couldn't control my weight. I'd never had a weight problem before and was always more slender than most, but on a team filled with skinny girls, you didn't want to risk being the biggest one—ever!

"Indi, I still eat whatever I want," Monique had said, pulling me aside after practice one day. "I just simply stick my finger down my throat and throw up. That way I can still eat whatever I want and the pounds don't stick."

At first I thought she was crazy—crazy like the man who stood in front of the BP gas station begging for change and having a full-blown conversation with himself. Monique was thinner than me and worried about gaining weight. But after I thought about it, I figured there must be some truth to what she was saying. After all, she was a returning dancer, a junior, so she'd been on the team for a while. She even told me about a girl who had gotten kicked off the team because she gained too much weight. So I took her advice to heart. I soon discovered that I could eat whatever I wanted and not pick up one single pound. And nobody ever had to know.

I washed my face, brushed my teeth and swished mouthwash around in my mouth. I thought about pulling my math book out again and making the changes that Marcus suggested, but I decided against it. They were changes I could make in my home room class in the morning, or I could rush and do them on the school bus on the way to school. I had time and I had options.

Thoughts of Marcus filled my head as I lay flat on my bed, staring at the ceiling and wondering what was wrong with me. Wasn't he attracted to me? Maybe he saw the same pounds that Monique saw—the ones that I'd picked up over the holidays.

"Indi." I barely heard Mama calling me, until she pushed my bedroom door open. "Indi, telephone."

I sat up in bed. "Who is it?"

"It's Jade," she said, handing me the cordless telephone.

Jade? Why was she calling me on the house phone? I grabbed the phone, but began feeling around for my cell phone. I checked the pocket of my coat and dug deep into my backpack. No phone. Must've left it at Marcus's.

"Hello."

"What's up, Ugly?"

"Right back at you."

"What's up with some dude answering your cell phone?"

"Marcus answered my phone?"

"He was very sweet and polite." Jade laughed.

"Ooh, I can't believe he answered my phone. That's an invasion of my privacy!" I screamed.

"Chill out, Indi. It's really not that serious."

"Yes, it is," I said through clenched teeth. "I would never answer his phone. He got some nerve. You wait till I see him."

"Well, if you're done trippin'—guess where I am."

"Where?" I asked, my anger subsiding a little.

"In the A-T-L, girl!"

"What? Why? How?" My mouth dropped open.

"My mother sent me here to live with my daddy for a while."

"Are you for real?"

"I'm for real. My daddy's apartment is about a mile from where you live."

"Can you come over?" I asked.

"He said not on a school night," Jade said. "But I'll be at school tomorrow. He enrolled me today."

"For real? You'll be at *my* high school tomorrow?"

"No, I'll be at *our* high school tomorrow." Jade giggled. "Hey, you think I can talk to your dance coach about getting on the team?"

"I don't know. Tryouts were pretty intense. And some girls got eliminated," I said, thinking how cool that would be if she was on the dance team. "But we can always ask."

"Let's do that," Jade said. I could hear the smile and excitement in her voice.

"My locker is on the third floor. Locker number 327. Can you meet me there before first period in the morning?"

"I'll be there, Ugly." She laughed. "Now go get your phone from your man."

"I plan to."

"And, Indi," she said, "go easy on the brother. He sounds sweet."

"Whatever," I said. "I'll see you tomorrow."

I hung up and pressed the phone to my chest. I

smiled. My best friend was back. I had a sweet boy-friend, who was also smart—even though I was mad at him at the moment. I was on the dance team. My grades were decent. And now my best friend was back in town—to stay!

Life was pretty good.

CHAPTER 3

Marcus

why was I sweating Mr. Smith's science test? I was good at science. It was one of my favorite subjects next to math, but something about the test had me afraid to go to sleep before I studied just one more time. I thought I was ready, but he had a few trick questions on the last one and I came real close to getting a D. He was so arrogant, too, with his polyester suit—the one that looked as if he had it since the seventies or eighties. I bet he grew up in my pop's era. A time and place when people wore Jheri curls, did break-dancing moves and listened to Kurtis Blow and Run-D.M.C.

Yep, that was definitely my pop's era. His and Gloria's, my Step-Mommy-Dearest. Or, should I say, my father's wife. She was definitely an unwelcome fixture in my world. After my parents divorced two years ago, I ended up living with my pop and Gloria. My biological mother lived in Houston, and constantly made promises that she never kept, especially the ones about sending for me. I'd long stopped putting my heart into her promises, because all they seemed to do was crush me each time she didn't come through. Now she was considering marrying some dude that she met in Houston. Even had the nerve to put him on the phone on Christmas Day when I last talked to her. He must've thought I was eight years old or something, because he kept asking me what Santa had brought me for Christmas. Now how stupid is that? It's been years since I stopped believing that some fat white dude was responsible for my Christmas gifts. It was a dude, alright, but his name definitely wasn't Santa Claus. His name was Rufus Carter—my pop.

Pop used to be my best friend—that is, until Gloria came along. I didn't have many friends. There were only a handful of guys my age that I could actually have an intelligent conversation with. Most of the guys in my neighborhood and at my school were into other things: selling dope, smoking dope, mistreating girls, skipping school—all the things I wasn't interested in. There were a few that weren't into those things, but they were nerds. And I definitely wasn't a nerd, either. And because I didn't fit in with either crowd, it caused me to be a misfit. And misfits just don't have many friends. They sit around in their bedroom, studying for tests that they're afraid they might flunk. And they think about their girlfriend, and how they want to steal her virginity, but then the good guy in them shows up and wants to slow things down a pace. That's what misfits like me did.

Indigo Summer caused me to feel things that I'd never felt before. She made me sing off-key in the shower—love songs, too, like Marcus Houston's "My Favorite Girl." And she made me go out for the basketball team, even though I had given up on sports. She had me up in the wee hours of the night, wondering if she was up in the wee hours of the night thinking about me, too. And when I kissed her lips, I actually felt this fluttering inside my heart. Kinda like it might explode or something. The first time I felt it, I wanted to ask Pop about it but didn't want him to worry or to think I was a punk or anything. Because I'm not a punk and I would never admit that I saw sparks whenever Indigo came my way. Never. And never would I ever tell her how I really felt. That I was falling—whatever that meant. I couldn't go out like that.

She was ready to take the relationship to the next

level. I could tell. The last couple of times we were together, she seemed so aggressive, so hungry for more than a kiss. But my hormones and my brain weren't on the same page, and until I could get both of them in sync with each other, I wasn't willing to go there. Going to the next level with someone was huge, not something to be taken lightly. Especially since I really cared about her. There were girls in my past that I didn't think twice about getting with. As long as I practiced safe sex and was responsible, there weren't any other reservations. But with Indigo it was different. I wanted it to be right. She was special.

I shut my science book. I had studied all that I could, and just prayed to God that I aced this test. At least score a B-minus or better. That was my goal. I pumped my last few reps of iron, and then strolled over to my window to see if Indigo's bedroom light was still on. Her room was dark; she must've fallen fast asleep after going off on me for accidentally answering her cell phone. She left it over here and it rang, so I picked it up on impulse. I wasn't being nosey, or "checking up on her," as she put it. I don't know why I picked it up. I couldn't even explain. But what's done is done. If she wanted to be mad about something so small, then let her.

I grabbed the bag of Skittles from my computer

desk, emptied a few into my palm, lifted my window and threw one at Indigo's bedroom window. It took a few throws before her light finally came on. She lifted her blinds, and then her window.

"Yes?" she asked with this sister-girl attitude, her hands on her small hips. She was so beautiful, with her wild hair and pretty smile. She was even cuter when she was angry.

"You still mad?" I asked.

"And what if I am, Marcus?"

"Then you should stop," I said. "It's not that serious."

"It's serious to me. You invaded my privacy."

"Fine, Indi. I said I was sorry."

"Did you study for your science test?" she asked, changing the subject and letting her guard down a little.

"Yeah. But I don't think I'm ready."

"You'll do fine, boy. You always stressing for no reason." She smiled, and I was so happy to see that smile show back up. It meant she wasn't mad anymore. "Guess what?" she asked.

"What?"

"My best friend Jade is back in town. She lives here now."

"Really?"

"Yep. She's supposed to meet me at my locker in the morning before first period. Man, I haven't seen her since last summer."

"That's cool, Indi. I'm happy for you. I know how tight you and Jade used to be."

"Yeah, man, since elementary school!" The excitement in her voice made me smile. I wanted good things for Indigo.

"Cool, well get some rest," I said. "I'll holler at you in the morning. You riding with me?"

"Yes."

"Be on time, Indi. I'm leaving at seven forty-five sharp. That doesn't mean for you to come running out of the house, half-dressed, carrying a Pop-Tart at seven-fifty. I'm leaving at seven forty-five."

"Whatever, Marcus."

"I'm serious, girl. Be on time." I raised an eyebrow and gave her a serious look. "I'ma leave you if you're late."

"You ain't leaving me," she sassed, with her hand on her hip again.

"I'ma leave you. You watch."

"Yeah, *you* watch."

"Good night, Indi."

"Good night, Marcus." She blew me a kiss and then shut her window.

"I love you." I whispered it after she was gone. I wasn't brave enough to say it out loud just yet.

I blew her a kiss, too.

CHAPTER 4

Jade

MY heart pounded as I roamed the halls of my new high school. It pounded so loudly that I could actually hear it. I'd missed Indigo all morning, too busy trying to find my classes. That was a chore in itself. It wasn't until the afternoon that I finally spotted her. I took two steps at a time until I reached the third floor. She was standing in the middle of the hallway, cheesing and waving. I would have to teach that girl how to be more cool and low-key. She had a lot of growing up to do. She still had that little-girl thing going on. We would definitely have to do something about that before the end of the school year.

"What's up, Ugly?" I had to admit, it was nice seeing my girl again. We had been tighter than tight and I couldn't wait for us to hang out again. Indigo was like family.

"What's up?" She stood in the middle of the floor like a rap artist, with her hands folded across her chest—being silly.

We hugged and I put her in a semi-headlock. Then I stepped back to get a good look at my friend who I hadn't seen in several months. The girl I remembered was smaller. She looked as if she'd gained a few pounds. Not many, but it was noticeable.

"Girl, what's up with those hips? Are you gaining weight or what?"

"You can tell?"

"A little bit." I laughed. "It's a good thing, though. You used to be a bean pole. But not anymore." I moved in closer and whispered in her ear. "Is Marcus knocking the boots?"

"No!" she yelled and pushed my shoulder. "Shut up, girl."

"I'm just asking 'cause you know what they say. When you start knocking boots, your hips start spreading. People can tell."

"I'm still a virgin, Jade."

"For real?" I asked. "But you'll tell me when that changes, right?"

"Come on. Let me help you find your class." Indigo totally ignored me and changed the subject.

Sex was a subject that we'd talked about a million times and promised that we'd let each other know the minute "it" happened for either of us. If one of us did it first, we'd let the other know immediately. That was our pact. But I'd totally broken the pact because I hadn't told her about my first and only time. An experience that was hurtful and degrading. No, I hadn't told her anything about that. I guess what she didn't know wouldn't hurt her.

She grabbed her book out of her locker and slammed it shut. We began to stroll down the hall. A beautiful creature with light brown eyes passed by us in the hallway, locked eyes with Indigo and grinned from ear to ear.

"Hey, Indi, what's up?" he asked and had me wondering who he was.

"What's up?" Indigo asked dryly.

"Hello there." I pushed Indigo out of the way and held my hand out to this brother wearing a red Falcons jersey—my favorite color. He was way too fine for her to be so nonchalant about him. If she wasn't interested, I certainly was. "I'm Jade. And you are?"

"Quincy." He took my hand in his. "Quincy Rawlins."

"Oh, it's you." I dropped my smile and pulled my hand away.

"What's that supposed to mean? *Oh, it's you?*" he asked, obviously not aware that Indigo had told me all about his trifling behind.

"Never mind," I said. Leaving Quincy in the middle of the hallway, I grabbed Indigo's arm. "Come on, Indi, we gotta get to class."

Quincy Rawlins was her infamous ex-boyfriend. The one who'd dumped her for some girl named Patrice on Christmas Day. In my book, he was a sleazebag and didn't even deserve to speak to her. However, during my first and very brief encounter with him, I had already determined that he *was* fine. I could see why she'd fallen head over heels for him in the first place. The boy had it going on. He was all that and a bag of chips, especially wearing those jeans. I couldn't wait to see Marcus—hadn't seen him since we were in elementary school, when he moved away. I barely remembered him. Apparently he had changed since then. If he was even half as cute as Quincy, then he was fine, too!

Boys always did make a big fuss over Indigo. She was cute, slender and somewhat reserved. Not like me. I was far from being reserved. Sometimes I just said exactly what was on my mind. Why keep people guessing? That's what I say. That way you leave no room for misunderstanding. If people know where you stand, they can't play their little games with you. Everything's on the table. My daddy told me once that when you say everything that's on your mind, it takes away your mystery. Who wants to be mysterious anyway?

I always considered myself mediocre when it came to looks. And my slender days were long over. I wasn't fat or anything, just not skinny. The women at my grandmother's church called me overdeveloped for my age.

"That girl is shaped just like a grown woman," one of them said. She thought she was whispering, but not softly enough, because I heard every word she said.

"These girls nowadays are just as fast as they wanna be," said the other woman, who wasn't whispering at all. "She'll be pregnant before she graduates high school."

I was just about to give her a piece of my mind, but my mama happened to walk up at the same time, smiled curtly at the women, and then ushered me on out the door. Good thing, because I would've been repenting to the Lord for two months for what I was about to say. She didn't know anything about me. She didn't know if I was sexually active or not—and then passing judgment on me like that. She didn't know about the one time that I had sex with a boy who promised to love me forever and ever.

Jarrod Michaels had made me feel like I was special. Most boys didn't give me a second look, but he did. That is until he got what he wanted from me. Then he never looked my way again. That hurt. Hurt for a long time. But I wasn't worried. Someday I would find someone to love me for me. Someday soon, I hoped.

The bell rang just as I bid Indigo a farewell and stepped into my history class. Everyone was already seated as I tiptoed to the back of the room to take my place in the only empty seat next to the wall.

"You must be Miss Morgan." The teacher, wearing a crisp white dress shirt and a colorful tie, stood and walked closer to my desk. He was much younger than any of the teachers I remembered in middle school or at my high school in Jersey.

"Yes. I'm Jade," I said as I plopped down in my seat, my book slamming against the wooden desktop.

"Very nice for you to join us, Jade," he said, smiling. "But I have to tell you that you are late if you're not already in your seat before the bell rings. I do understand that this is your first day, but when you attend my class, you must be on time."

I looked at him like he was crazy. Was he waiting for me to say something?

"Do I make myself clear?" Now that was a question and he was really expecting an answer. I could tell by the way his eyes stared into mine until I broke the stare. I looked around the room at all the other faces staring back at me, each one anticipating my response. The whole class looked my way, and I was sure that if I didn't say something quick, they'd all jump me.

"I understand," I finally whispered.

"I'm sorry, I didn't hear you."

"I understand." I said it louder and wanted to slap that smug look off of his face.

"Good," he said, smiling again. "So tomorrow I can expect to see you in your chair, a bright shining smile on your face, with your book opened and ready to learn before the bell rings. Am I correct?"

"Exactly," I said sarcastically, and waited for him to walk away. As soon as he turned his back, I flipped up my middle finger toward the back of his head. Who did he think he was anyway? Was it written in the school's book of rules somewhere that we had to be seated before the bell rang? Surely that was some stupid rule that he'd made up. And what were the consequences if you didn't abide by this made-up piece of crap?

As snickers echoed across the room from students who thought my flipping him off was funny, Mr. Whatever-His-Name-Was turned around.

"You don't wanna find out what happens to students who have a problem getting to my class on time," he said as if he'd read my mind. He seemed to be speaking to the entire class but his eyes landed on me. "So, do you have a joke you would like to share with the class, Miss Morgan?"

"No," I said innocently.

"Good," he said. I was grateful that he turned away, walked toward the blackboard again and began writing some stuff on it in white chalk.

I reached into the pocket of my three-ring binder and pulled out my crumpled-up schedule. Who was this dude? I wanted to know his name. I read the words on the page: Mr. Steven Collins, American History, Room 325. He had chocolate-brown skin with a bald head and shiny white teeth. He was tall and slender, almost cute. How could someone who looked like that be so uptight? What a waste, I thought as I settled into my chair, got comfortable and opened my history book to the page he was teaching from. This was going to be a long semester if he didn't loosen up a bit.

CHAPTER 5

Indigo

As Jay-Z's "Show Me What You Got" rang through the gym, I swayed my hips to the music. Got lost in the rhythm of it. I glanced into the stands and Jade was swaying her hips, too. She was actually trying to show my dance coach, Miss Martin, that she could dance, in hopes that she would change her mind about letting her on the team. She had already cornered Miss Martin before practice and asked her if she had room for one more girl.

"Sorry, sweetheart, I have all the girls I need," Miss Martin had said and then continued to write something on her clipboard. Jade had been dismissed, but didn't know it.

"But I can really dance," she'd said.

"I'm sure you can, young lady, you and half the student body. But first of all, I have all the girls I need on the team. And secondly, to become a member of this dance team, you must go through intense tryouts that already took place last semester. I have a long waiting list of girls awaiting their shot on the team."

"All that's cool, ma'am, but you haven't seen me dance," Jade continued.

Miss Martin sighed and held her clipboard at her side. "Okay, let me see what you got," she finally said.

Without any music, except the music in her head, Jade started to move. She swayed her hips and moved her body like she was in a video. It looked like a routine that she'd already practiced a million times because it was flawless. I stared at Jade and glanced at Miss Martin to see if I could figure out what she was thinking, then I looked back at Jade. With moves like that, how could she tell her no? I closed my eyes and crossed my fingers until Jade finally placed her hands on her hips and took a bow. The boys in the stands were going crazy. The other girls on the team clapped and slapped high fives with Jade. They seemed to like her already and whispered about how good a dancer she was. I hugged her.

"That was very nice, Jade, thank you," Miss Martin

said before lifting her clipboard and turning her back on Jade to face the rest of us. "Okay, ladies, let's get started."

Jade had been dismissed again. Her eyes questioned me and I shrugged my shoulders. Miss Martin was different. She had to love Jade's routine. How could she not? But she wasn't offering her a place on the team. She just asked us to line up so that we could practice our new routine. Jade folded her arms across her chest and with a frown on her face found a seat on the bleachers. After studying our routine, she soon had it memorized as she moved her hips right along with the team. I felt sorry for her. Wished that she hadn't moved away in the first place. She belonged on this team. She knew it, I knew it and so did Miss Martin. But there was nothing that any of us could do about it. There was a waiting list of girls ahead of Jade, wishing they were on the team. She didn't stand a chance.

As my father's pickup pulled up in front of Jade's apartment complex, she gazed out of the window at the unit that she now shared with her father. The blinds were opened, but the apartment was pitch-black, which meant her father wasn't home. She dug into her Baby Phat purse and pulled out a huge set of keys. There were about five keys on the ring, a rabbit's foot, a whistle, a picture of her little sister, Mattie, a key chain that read "Nassau, Bahamas" that her aunt brought her back from vacation. Her set of keys took up about two-thirds of the space in her purse. She held the key to her apartment in the air.

"I can get in," she said, smiling at my daddy, who seemed uneasy about dropping her off and leaving her there. "My daddy will be home soon."

"Indi, why don't you walk her upstairs," he said.

I unsnapped my seat belt and the two of us jumped out of the truck. We jogged up the stairs two at a time. The winter chill brushed across my face as I pulled my bubble coat tighter. My Mudd jeans hugged my hips and I suddenly wished I had worn tights underneath. The patter of Jade's black suede Pumas and my red-and-white Filas played a tune on the wooden stairs until we reached the top. As we approached her door, I heard voices inside. I stopped in my tracks and gave Jade a cockeyed look that said, "What's up with the voices?"

She must have read my mind because she started laughing.

"My daddy leaves the radio on. He says that it makes people think that somebody's at home. Keeps 'em from breaking into our house."

"Oh," was all I could say as my pounding heart slowed back down to its normal speed.

Jade turned her key in the lock and opened the door. She flipped the switch on the wall by the door to turn on the light. "I would invite you in, but I know your daddy's waiting."

"It's cool. I'll see if I can come over this weekend."

"Yeah, do that. Some boys who live in Building Three are having a party on Saturday night. They were talking about it in my math class today." She removed her backpack from her shoulder and dropped it in the middle of the floor.

"Okay, I better go before my daddy starts blowing his horn," I said. "I'll see you tomorrow."

"Alright, Ugly," she said. "I'll come to your locker in the morning."

"Cool," I said before jogging down the wooden stairs, my Filas playing that tune again. An older woman on the second level peeped through her blinds at me, and snapped them shut when my eyes met hers. I jumped into my daddy's truck, snapping my seat belt tight around me.

"Can I spend the night with Jade on Friday night, Daddy?" I just went ahead and put it out there. Got it out in the open, just to see what I was working with. He seemed to be in a good mood, and the apartment complex seemed safe. Not to mention Jade was like family. She had been my best friend for so long, and our families had lived next door to each other for years. Our fathers had watched a million football games together and drank just as many beers. Our mothers had shopped at Wal-Mart together on many occasions and had taken us to the mall more times than I could count. Jade's family had spent Christmases at our house and ate barbecued ribs with us on the Fourth of July. My father had sprayed us both down with the water hose and I can't even count the number of times I'd had fried chicken at Jade's house. Yes, they were family. Surely he wouldn't say no.

"Indi, I don't know. Things are a little different now that it's just Jade and Ernest. It's a little awkward for me."

"What's awkward about it, Daddy? You know Mr. Ernest. You've known him for years." What was he talking about? This was our family he was feeling awkward about.

"We'll talk to your mama," he said. "See what she says."

Talk to Mama? Was he serious? If he was thinking this way, her thoughts would be ten times worse. I could forget about spending the weekend with Jade and about the party in Building Three.

Yet, I still hoped for a miracle.

CHAPTER 6

Marcus

how did I get so lucky? Being nominated, against my will I might add, to be the math tutor to Carver's very own starting center, Kent Carpenter. Kent Carpenter, basketball player extraordinaire with the prettiest dunk I'd ever seen. He had played varsity since he was a freshman. I was sure that his six-foot-two-inch frame had a lot to do with his ability to literally snatch the ball from his opponents' hands and block their shots with so much aggression, they wanted to beat his behind. But nobody ever tried. It was a losing battle. He was a bully and let the world know it every time they thought they wanted to step to him. He caused teachers to think twice.

Nonetheless, I was assigned to teach this dude algebra, which he didn't have a clue about or an interest in. I wondered how he'd been promoted since the ninth grade. It definitely wasn't because he'd applied himself and made the grades. Now here he was, a senior in high school, scouts jocking him for college, and he was failing tenth-grade algebra even though he was a senior. According to my sources, he was barely skinning by in American history, literacy and Spanish, too. The only class that he made good grades in was gym. And even there, he refused to dress out, claiming that he had some sort of condition. Most times, the faculty just let him do whatever he wanted because he was the team's star player. A lot of the benefits he received in life were because of his position on the basketball team. The cheerleaders made sure he passed all of his tests, and the groupies, the ones who followed basketball players around, completed his homework assignments. I bet he hadn't completed one assignment on his own since ninth grade, and probably couldn't tell you a thing that he learned since then. He made passing grades because of other people.

He kept talking about his dreams of going to the NBA, and that he didn't need a college education for that. He just needed his pretty jump shot, and that dunk of his that had people in the stands screaming their heads off. Yep, as long as he had that, who needed school? He had it all worked out in his mind. I even remember asking him how he was going to read over his million-dollar contract if he couldn't read.

"I'll have people who can do that, Marcus. Lawyers and stuff," he'd said.

"How you gon' count your money if you can't count?" I came back with.

"I'll have an accountant for that."

"Somebody you can trust, right?" I asked sarcastically.

"Of course, somebody I can trust."

"That's cool. At least you can trust them not to steal from you. Make sure it's somebody like that," I said, trying to get him to see my point.

He had totally missed it.

Here I was in the school's library, checking my watch every two minutes, waiting for Mr. Star Center to show up. He was already ten minutes late and my patience was running thin. He had five minutes to show up, after which I was heading to my Jeep and burning rubber out of the parking lot. He was imposing on my time that I normally spent with Indigo, helping *her* with math while trailing kisses up and down her neck. Trying to get her to focus when it seemed that her mind was somewhere else: places where I wasn't sure she or I was ready for—places that changed relationships forever. She had been talking to some of her girlfriends and had convinced herself that she was ready to lose her virginity. I wasn't ready for our relationship to change, but peer pressure seemed to demand that we take it to the next level. This was something that had me daydreaming in class, missing the lesson I was supposed to get. But I couldn't help it; she was in my thoughts every day—like crazy! Even when I tried to brush her away, she was still there.

Kent stood at the entrance of the library, his foot holding the door open as Brianna Douglas wrapped her skinny arms tightly around his neck. Her lips pressed against his; it was clear they were French-kissing while his hands roamed all over her body. Miss Anderson, the media specialist, peered over the top of her black-rimmed glasses at the sight, but never opened her lips to say a word. She just shook her head and gave them a look of disgust as Brianna pried her lips from Kent's. He winked at Miss Anderson as he strolled over to where I was seated.

"I bet Miss Anderson would love to get a piece of me." He grinned. "Look at her over there, checking me out. I bet behind those ugly glasses is a beautiful woman with a bodacious body like Beyoncé's."

"Man, you are sick." The thought of Miss Anderson in that way made me frown.

"I'm serious," he said and then winked at Miss Anderson. She didn't seem to mind the attention Kent was giving her and I wondered if she would really allow a student to seduce her.

"Yo, man, I ain't got all day," I said, opening my algebra book to chapter twelve.

"Me neither," he said, pulling a chair from the table and stretching his long legs out as he straddled the chair backwards. "Let's get this over with."

"Where's your math book, dog?" I asked.

"Left it in my locker. You didn't tell me I needed to bring it."

Common sense would tell you that, I wanted to say. But what I said was, "Whatever, man. Did you even attempt to work through the problems?"

"That's what I got you for, man, to help me work through the problems."

I could see that this was going to be an interesting afternoon and it was clear to me that I needed to let this brother know who he was dealing with.

"Look, man, let me tell you something. Coach asked me to tutor you in order to help bring your grade up to passing. I'm on the basketball team, too, and I'm passing all my classes."

"What's your point, punk?" he asked, hostile now.

"My point is I don't need to be here in the library trying to tutor somebody in math, man, who don't wanna be tutored! I got mine. I'm trying to help you." I was serious. "I also got better things to do with my time."

"So go do 'em," he said.

"Cool, I will," I said. I closed my book and stuffed it into my backpack, which I threw over my shoulder. I stood up. "Later."

"You really gon' walk away like that?" He smiled. "You must not know who I am, man."

He obviously wasn't used to people standing up to him because he seemed to be shocked at my reaction.

"I know exactly who you are. Kent Carpenter, the brother who can run rings around his opponents on the basketball court, but don't even care enough about his own education to apply himself."

"Whoa! I care about my education, man. I'm going to the University of Illinois—" he pretended to throw his famous jump shot, as if he was on the court "—or maybe I'll go to Georgia State, or maybe even UCLA. I don't know—I have so many options."

"So many options, but you can't even read the application in order to apply."

"Screw you, man! I don't need to read no application. I'm getting a basketball scholarship—a free ride, punk! Something that you wouldn't know nothing about."

Before I knew it, Kent was in my face with his fingers wrapped around my neck.

"You got five seconds to get your hands off of me." I strained my voice just to speak.

"Or what, punk?"

Or what? I didn't have an answer for that. I hadn't thought that question through and was at a loss for words. My heart pounded so loud I could hear it in my ears. But I didn't back down. I had principles. Miss Anderson stood, as if she was about to come over and rescue me.

"Look, man, if you want to skate through high school and never learn anything, that's on you. But you're only hurting yourself. These teachers don't care if you get yours or not. Well, maybe a few of them, but most of them don't. They just here for a paycheck. You have to want it for yourself."

Something I said must've caught his attention because he let go of my neck.

"I don't need algebra and science and all this other crap, man. I'm going to the pros."

"And who will you trust to read your contract for

you before you sign it?" It was like déjà vu, because I could've sworn we'd had this conversation before.

"I'll have an attorney to read it and explain it to me," he said and sat back down. "What's up with you, dude? Are you always this uptight?"

"I'm not uptight, I just don't like wasting my time."

"You sound like one of my teachers, man."

"I'm not trying to," I said, then adjusted my backpack over my shoulder again and started toward the door.

"Hey, wait, man. If I don't pass this test on my own, I get kicked off the team," he said.

"Yeah, so?" I turned around and looked at him.

"So I need your help," he said, sort of mumbling. "I ain't got my book, but I can use yours, right?"

He wasn't so tough now that I was ready to walk away. I stood there for a moment and thought about it.

"Yeah, you can use mine." I walked back over to the table, placed my backpack in a chair and pulled my math book back out again. "But let me tell you, man, if I'm gonna be your tutor, you need to respect my time."

He was silent.

"I'm only giving you a five-minute grace period, and then I'm gone, man, I'm telling you." I opened the book to chapter twelve again and slid the book across the table to Kent. "And you need to bring your book with you next time, and any assignments that you get in class."

"You really are serious about this stuff, huh?"

"I'm very serious."

"I'm talking about math—you're serious about math."

"I'm serious about my education, period. Nobody cares if I pass or fail, except for me. I have to get this for me because I don't wanna be working at Burger King for the rest of my life."

"I feel you, man," he said with my open book in front of him. "I feel you."

What had I gotten myself into?

CHAPTER 7

Jade

I sat in the middle of my canopy bed, my books spread out all over it, Bow Wow and Chris Brown singing "Shorty Like Mine" on the small clock radio on my nightstand. The smell of burnt macaroni and cheese still lingered in my dad's small apartment. The directions said to let it simmer, but I must've missed that part the first time I read them because I had the stove turned all the way up. It hadn't taken long for all of the water to evaporate, the macaroni to stick to the bottom of the pan and the fire alarm to start chirping out of control. After sending macaroni down the garbage disposal, I made myself a bowl of Froot Loops and called that dinner.

It was already dark outside, the streetlights creeping

through my window, and Daddy still wasn't home. I guess I wasn't prepared for his late hours. He was never home and not only was I lonely most nights, but I was scared sometimes, too. I kept hearing noises in the other rooms of the apartment, like a tapping sound in the kitchen. And the sound of footsteps in the stairwell always caused my heart to beat faster than a normal pace, wondering if somebody was about to pound on the door. By the time I heard Daddy's key in the keyhole most nights, I'd already fallen asleep and had awakened at least three times.

What happened to the quality time we were supposed to be spending together?

Tonight he was a little earlier than he was most nights. I listened as his key turned in the lock and laughter followed. Not just his laughter, but a woman's giggle, too. I sat still, trying to make out the muffled voices and giggles coming from the living room. Then the bass from Marvin Gaye's old-school song "Trouble Man" echoed through the apartment, drowning out my clock radio. I waited to hear Daddy's footsteps in the hallway, until he suddenly appeared in the doorway of my room.

"Hey, baby girl." He had that look. The one he gets when he's had a few beers.

"Hi, Daddy." I smiled at him. His tie was undone

and the jacket of his suit was barely hanging on to his arms.

"What's that burning smell?" he asked, frowning.

"I tried making myself some mac and cheese." I laughed. "Guess I didn't read the directions all the way through."

"I'm sorry, baby. I should've brought you something to eat. We'll go grocery shopping tomorrow for some real food." He looked worried. "Are you hungry?"

"I had a bowl of cereal."

"Good," he said. "Why don't you come on in the living room? Got somebody I want you to meet."

"Who?" I was curious now as I slipped big fuzzy house shoes on my feet.

"You'll see. Come on."

I followed Daddy down the hallway and into the living room. My eyes landed on the woman seated on the leather couch in the living room, her face the color of vanilla, her hair in a short, sassy style. Her business suit reminded me of the ones they wore at my dad's office.

"Baby, this is Veronica." Daddy grinned from ear to ear. "Veronica, this is my baby girl, Jade. Jade, say hello."

I was speechless as I stared at this woman who I instantly couldn't stand. Why was she in our apartment trying to date my daddy anyway? Didn't she know it was just a matter of time before my mother moved back to Atlanta and into our apartment? It was my goal in life to reunite my family. Didn't she know that? I looked away in order to keep from glaring at her. And I kept my mouth closed in order to keep from being disrespectful.

"Jade, where's your manners? Say hello." Daddy's grin turned into a frown.

"Hello," I mumbled, but still didn't look at her. Instead, I stared at my big fuzzy slippers.

"I've heard so much about you, Jade. Ernest tells me that you're a dancer."

"Yes, ma'am." It took everything in me just to get those two words out.

"Veronica was once a ballerina." Daddy's smile was back. "Ain't that right, babe?"

Did he just call her babe?

"Yes, that's right, Ernest." She smiled at my father and their eyes locked. "But that was many moons ago. I was much younger then and much thinner."

My dad cocked his head to the side as if he was evaluating her size and trying to imagine her much thinner. He grinned.

"Show us some of your moves, Jade," Daddy said.

Was he serious? Who could dance to grown folks' music, except for grown folks?

"To this?" I asked, as Marvin Gaye crooned.

"No. Go get one of your CDs, baby, and let us see you dance."

"Daddy, I'm kinda tired right now." I forced a yawn, and covered my mouth. "May I be excused? I have to get up pretty early."

He looked disappointed. Didn't want to let me off that easy, but how could he argue with a kid wanting to get herself ready for school?

"Okay, baby. Go on to bed." He held his arms out for a hug and I rushed into them. He planted a kiss on my cheek that reeked of alcohol.

"Good night, Daddy."

"Good night, baby."

"Good night, Jade," that woman said. "It was very nice meeting you."

"Good night," I said. To say that it was nice meeting her would've been a lie, so I kept it simple.

Once inside my bedroom, I fell onto the bed face-down and buried my head in the pillow. Things weren't going as planned.

I needed a Plan B, and fast.

As the bell sounded, I tiptoed to the back of the classroom, praying Mr. Collins didn't turn around until I was seated. I'd tried with everything in me to get to his class on time, but it was next to impossible.

"Miss Morgan."

"Yes?" I rolled my eyes at the ceiling and then turned to face Mr. Collins.

"Miss Morgan, you must not have heard me clearly yesterday when I explained the rules of this classroom to you."

"I heard you," I said, "but, Mr. Collins, it's hard trying to get here on time and to be in my seat and all that before the bell rings."

"If you cut your conversations in the hallway short—" he approached as I slid into my desk "—then it can be done."

I slowly inhaled and then exhaled.

"Sorry," I mumbled.

"Consider this a warning, Miss Morgan," he said before turning away and heading back to the front of the class. "Next time, you'll be serving a detention."

I nodded, but made a mental note to check with the administration about Mr. Collins's rule. Surely he couldn't get away with this. As I looked around at all the other students seated at their desks like soldiers, I wondered if any of them had ever challenged this dude.

Didn't anyone in here have a backbone? I thought, as the chocolate boy three rows over smiled at me, his teeth perfect and white. I smiled back. He was kind of cute with his long sideburns and perfectly trimmed goatee. He seemed too old to be in a freshman American history class.

"Now if you'll all find a partner for today's exercise," Mr. Collins said.

Before I knew it, Chocolate Boy was at my desk.

"You got a partner?" he asked, flashing those pearly whites again.

"I guess it's you, partner," I said and he immediately plopped down at the desk next to mine.

I couldn't help thinking he was a juvenile delinquent or a gang member…or maybe he was gay. That would be the only reason someone like that would consider talking to someone like me. Yes, he had to be one of those things.

"You're cute, Miss—what does he call you? Miss Morgan." He mocked our teacher, Mr. Collins. "I'm Terrence."

"Just call me Jade," I said and opened my book to the page that Mr. Collins was telling us to turn to. "How do you get here on time?"

"My class before this one is right next door," Terrence said.

"Oh. That makes it easy for you," I said. "I have gym, and you know how far that is."

"It's cool. Just tell your gym teacher that you have

Mr. Collins, and she'll let you leave a few minutes early."

"For real? Is it that serious?"

"Everybody around here knows he got issues," Terrence said. "What school did you transfer from?"

"I moved here from New Jersey."

"Oh," he said. "You going to that party on Friday night?"

"No doubt." I smiled, thinking about the party I'd been anticipating for a week.

"Cool. Maybe I'll see you there."

"Maybe you will," I said, still smiling.

Terrence seemed to be normal, I thought, as we shared our American history book and completed our assignment together.

CHAPTER 8

Indigo

It had been ages since I rode the bus. Usually after dance team practice, I rode home with Marcus or my daddy picked me up in front of the gym. But dance team practice had been cancelled because Miss Martin had an emergency. Daddy wasn't available to pick me up, and Marcus was headed to the library to tutor some stupid basketball player. So I found myself on the bus, peering out of the window, sitting next to Donald Long, who kept talking to me. He must not have known that his breath was so tart it was capable of starting a fire. And I didn't want to hurt his feelings by breaking the news to him. I just wished he would catch my drift and notice that I kept peering out of the window in an attempt to block the fire. Finally I offered him a piece of Big Red. He took it, popped it into his mouth, but still didn't catch the hint and continued to talk.

Kids were engaged in loud conversations about the party on Friday night. Everybody was talking about it and I hadn't even built up enough nerve to ask my mother if I could go yet. I was still trying to perfect my strategy. The plan was to spend the night at Jade's house, but that was next to impossible, considering she lived with her father and there was no woman in the house. How could I convince my folks that it was safe? That was the challenge. Where was Nana when I needed her? Nana Summer, my grandmother and dearest friend, was a woman that could out-dance some of my friends and whip some of the neighborhood kids in a game of one-on-one back in the day. She was much older now, and suffered from sugar diabetes and high blood pressure, but she was still as sharp as a tack and was so open-minded. She would understand my need to attend this party. Everybody who was anybody would be there. If you didn't show up, you might as well not show up at school on Monday morning. Everybody from the dance team would be there, the cheerleaders and all the basketball players. And if I played my cards right, I would be there, too.

After the bus pulled next to the curb, its tires screeching, Donald stood and let me out of my seat. I rushed to get off before he could say another word or offer to walk me to my door. I decided to jog down the block instead of just strolling. The Atlanta wind was brisk as it slapped against my face. The sooner I got inside the house and warmed up my fingertips the better. My Filas thumped against the wooden porch as I took two steps at a time and stuck my key in the door. I was greeted by the smell of my Nana's peach cobbler as I shut the door behind me. It was a distinct smell that couldn't be denied and for a minute I thought she might be at my house, but I knew Nana lived in Chicago and it wasn't likely she was there for a visit. She usually visited during holidays and the summertime, and it was neither of the two.

I dropped my backpack at the door and headed for the kitchen. If it was peach cobbler I smelled, there was no doubt that something else was waiting next to it on the stove, like some fried chicken or some pork chops smothered in gravy. I just followed my nose, and sure enough, there was a spread on the stove. It was like a Sunday dinner spread—fried chicken, mashed potatoes and corn-bread muffins—the works. What was the special occasion? I grabbed a paper towel and a chicken leg, looked around to make sure nobody was looking before I bit into it. Didn't want Mama slapping my hand and telling me to get out of her pots. But it was definitely a whole lot better than the peanut butter and jelly sandwich I was about to make.

"Well, well, well. Caught you red-handed."

I turned and found my Nana Summer standing in the doorway, hands on her round hips, her face the color of brown sugar.

"Nana! What are you doing here?" I asked and then ran into her arms. "When did you get here? How did you get here?"

"You're full of questions, ain't ya?" She laughed.

I missed my Nana when she wasn't around, and when she came to our house it was a special occasion. She usually spent the entire summer, Christmas and an occasional day or two, here or there. My father usually drove to Chicago and picked her up because she refused to get on an airplane. But I saw Daddy leave for work that morning and even if he drove to Chicago he wouldn't have been able to turn around and make the trip back that fast. Something was up, but I wasn't sure what.

"How did you get here?"

"I took the Greyhound." She shook her head. "The longest trip of my life."

"You took the Greyhound all the way from Chicago

to Atlanta, Nana? Why are you here? Why didn't you tell me you were coming?"

I talked to Nana on the phone at least three times a week and she had never mentioned that she was coming.

"I'm here because I wanna be," Nana said, and then grabbed two plates off of the shelf. "Sit down. Let's have some dinner."

I sat down at the kitchen table as Nana loaded our plates with soul food.

"Where's Mama?" I asked.

"She's upstairs resting," Nana said. "Can you pour us a couple of glasses of Kool-Aid, baby?"

"I'll pour myself a glass of Kool-Aid and you a glass of orange juice."

Nana frowned, but we both knew that sugar was not an option for her. She tried to get over every chance she got, but she forgot who she was talking to. I was both her sugar diabetes and her high blood pressure monitor. When she came to visit, I always made sure she ate the right things and drank the right things. Even though she didn't like it. She and I both knew that Kool-Aid had way too much sugar in it for her especially when *I* made the Kool-Aid. I loaded it down with sugar.

"Okay, orange juice," she said reluctantly.

"You'll thank me later, Nana." I smiled and pulled two glasses from the shelf. "It's because I love you."

"Yes, I love you, too. And a little Kool-Aid ain't never hurt nobody," she mumbled. "And I'm as grown as I can be."

I smiled and poured her a nice glass of orange juice. I poured myself one, too, just so she wouldn't feel alone, and wouldn't be eyeballing my Kool-Aid. I placed our glasses on the table as Nana set our plates next to them. I plopped down in my seat and she said grace. I couldn't wait for the amen, so I could dig in.

"I have something to tell you, baby," she said. "I need for you to be a grown-up right now."

A grown-up? That sounded serious.

"What is it?" She was worrying me.

"Your mama and daddy are having some real serious issues right now, Indi. Some marriage issues. They dealing with some heavy stuff."

"What kinda heavy stuff, Nana? Tell me."

"I can't share everything with you, baby. It's grown-folks stuff." Grown-folks stuff? Didn't she just tell me I was a grown-up? "Let's just say that they both are suffering right now."

"Are they getting a divorce, Nana?"

"I don't know, Indi. We're praying that it won't

come to that. That's why I'm here, to see if I can help them work through it. But I just don't know."

My heart began to pound rapidly at the thought that my parents might get a divorce. That couldn't be true. My parents loved each other too much. They had history together. They had me. And we were a family, and families just didn't break up. Whatever it was, we would get through it. I was sure of it.

Nana might as well have said somebody was dying because that's almost what it felt like.

"That explains why Mama's been crying all the time," I announced. "She wouldn't tell me what was wrong."

"She'll explain it to you when she's ready, baby," Nana said. "But for now, you just continue to be a good girl, stay out of trouble, do your chores and make good grades. Think you can handle that?"

"Yes, ma'am," I said and picked over my food. Suddenly my appetite was gone.

After dinner, Nana and I loaded the dishwasher and cleaned the countertops. We covered the food in aluminum foil and moved into the family room. Our favorite show, *American Idol,* was on and I didn't waste any time turning it on. However, first things first, I thought as I disappeared upstairs to my bathroom, my knees on the floor as I leaned over the toilet bowl. It wasn't long before I rid myself of every calorie that I'd eaten for dinner. After brushing my teeth and rinsing my mouth with mouthwash, I bounced back downstairs before Nana even noticed I was gone.

She was already relaxed in Daddy's recliner, her reading glasses at the tip of her nose as she watched *American Idol*. I stretched out in the middle of the floor in front of the television. I had homework, but it would have to wait until I saw what poor non-singing soul Simon, Randy and Paula would be sending home. Somebody was bound to get on there, claiming they could sing, and get their feelings hurt because their friends and family had lied to them all their lives. Told them they could sing, even though it was clear that they didn't have an ounce of talent.

As some girl with a voice that would make dogs howl in the middle of the night began to croon for the judges, my mind drifted to thoughts of my parents. I wondered what had happened that was so terrible that Nana Summer had to come all the way from Chicago. And for her to hop on a Greyhound bus, it had to be pretty serious. Something was definitely out of whack. What was happening to the Summer family? Were we going to end up like Jade's family, scattered across the United States like strangers? Would I stay with Mama or would

I live with Daddy? Who would get custody of me? Who would get the house? Would I end up with a stepmother like Marcus's? Or worse, a stepfather who couldn't stand me?

So many questions and not one single solitary answer.

CHAPTER 9

Marcus

tutoring Kent was draining all of my energy. He just didn't seem to get it, and I didn't know how to make it any clearer to him. I didn't want to write him off as a lost cause, but I was pretty close to it. He was more interested in talking about the girls at school and basketball plays than he was in studying for his algebra test. Most of the time it took everything in me just to keep him on task and today would be no different. Since the teachers were having a meeting in the library, we were running short on places to study. After much convincing, he finally agreed that his house was the closest and ideal place to go. He was reluctant but finally gave in.

As we pulled up in front of his house, I couldn't help thinking we had the wrong place. It was a small, dingy house on the corner of the street. It needed to be painted and the porch looked like it might cave in at any moment. It was getting late and although it wasn't quite dark outside, dusk was fast approaching. As we climbed the stairs of the small house, I entered cautiously, following behind Kent. Once inside, the curtains were drawn and the living room was dark. A woman sat on the sofa in the living room, a cigarette resting between her fingers, her legs crossed as she stared at—absolutely nothing.

"Hey, Ma," Kent said.

"'Bout time you got your behind home from school, boy. I told you I needed you to come straight home and not a minute after, Kent!" she yelled. "Told you I needed you to watch your little brother while I go to work. What's so hard about that, Kent?"

"Ma, I had basketball practice," he explained, as this little woman continued to yell at the top of her lungs. Why didn't she just stand out on the porch and shout it to the neighbors?

"I don't care about no basketball practice, boy! I'm trying to bring some money into this house so I can keep the lights and gas on, which is something that you should be helping me do. You need to get a job, Kent. I can't do this by myself. And your no-good daddy ain't giving me a dime to help out."

"Ma, I'm sorry," Kent said, hanging his head. He was a different person around his mother. He wasn't the same hardcore tough guy that he portrayed at school. "Why you sitting here in the dark?"

"You wanna know why I'm sitting here in the dark, Kent?" His mother stood and walked toward us. My back was close enough to the door that I could conveniently bolt to my car if need be. I thought she might hit him or something as she approached, but she reached for the light switch on the wall, which happened to be right next to my head, and began flipping it up and down. Up and down like a maniac. "I'm sitting here in the dark because the doggone lights are shut off, Kent. They turned the lights off because I couldn't pay the bill again this month. Last month it was the water, and the month before that the gas—in the dead of winter. That's why I'm sitting here in the dark! Because we ain't got no lights! And you're running around trying to be a basketball star instead of coming straight home like you're supposed to or finding a freakin' job like I asked you to."

"Sorry, Ma," Kent said, hanging his head again and I knew it was only because I was standing there that he didn't cry. He wanted to, I could tell.

"And who is this?" she asked, pointing her cigarette at me. "I done told you about bringin' strangers up in my house."

"This is Marcus Carter, Ma."

"Marcus Carter?" she said. "You Rufus Carter's boy?"

"Yes, ma'am," I said.

"Yo daddy is my landlord." I was surprised to see her smile. A very pretty smile that had been hidden by a frown and those wrinkles in her forehead. Her smile showed how pretty she was. "Yo daddy's a very nice man."

I didn't know what to say to that and just stood there. Shook my head in agreement. I looked around at the property that my father supposedly owned and wondered if he knew how run-down it was. Wondered if he'd evict them if he saw it.

"Marcus has been tutoring me in math, Ma," Kent explained.

"Hmmph. Tutoring you in math?" she asked. "You got a job, Marcus?"

"Yes, ma'am. I work at Burger King on the weekends," I said.

"See there, Kent, even this boy got a job. He need to be tutoring you in finding a job so you can help me pay these bills around here," she said, her short skirt creeping up above her thighs. "I'm about to go to work. I don't know what you gon' eat because there ain't nothing in there. But I'm sure you'll figure it out."

She grabbed her coat from the closet, wrapped up in it and headed out the door.

"Ma, where's Scottie?" Kent asked.

"He outside playing somewhere. You need to find him and figure out what y'all gon' eat for dinner."

She was gone and not fast enough, in my opinion.

Without lights, we definitely couldn't study at Kent's house, unless we intended to do it by candle-light. And I wasn't up for that.

"Well, I guess we can't study here," Kent said. The word *embarrassment* should've been written on his forehead.

"It's cool. We can go to my house," I said. "You and your little brother can just eat over there. I'm sure my stepmother got something she's cooked up. I can't promise that it will taste good, but at least it's a meal."

"Hey, we don't need your handouts, man. I'll figure something out," he said, quickly becoming defensive and putting up a wall.

"Cool, suit yourself, man," I said, heading out the door. "I'm going home."

He stood there on the front porch for a moment. His mind racing a million miles a minute, contemplating whether or not he should take me up on my offer or spend another night with a hungry, growling stomach.

"Wait. Let me find my brother and I'll follow you to your house."

I didn't know anyone stupid enough to pass up a free meal, especially when they didn't have any other options.

I pulled up in front of my house and shut my engine off. Kent's Honda pulled up behind my Jeep. I looked up at Indigo's window to see if her bedroom light was on. It was dark. Part of me wanted to ring her doorbell just to see a glimpse of her pretty face before I went into the house, but I didn't want her father, Mr. Summer, answering the door and asking me if I'd lost my mind. Then I'd have to explain what it was I wanted.

"I just wanna catch a glimpse of your daughter, Mr. Summer."

How stupid would that sound?

I'd missed hanging out with her after school and just wanted to see her beautiful smile. Would her father understand that?

I waited at the curb for Kent and his brother to step out of the car, and the three of us headed toward my porch. Inside, I led them straight for the kitchen, just to see what creative foods my stepmother, Gloria, had sitting on the stove. She was the worst cook in the world, in my opinion, and most of the time I would stop by McDonald's for a Big Mac prior to coming home. But tonight was a little different. I had three hungry mouths to feed, instead of just my own, and couldn't afford three Big Macs. I wasn't sure what was in the casserole dish on the stove, but it smelled like fish and didn't seem appetizing at all.

"Y'all want some of that?" I asked Kent and his brother. They both frowned, and I couldn't help laughing inside.

I reached for the loaf of bread and I made three peanut butter and jelly sandwiches as Kent and Scottie sat at the kitchen table. They ate the sandwiches so fast, I wondered when they had a meal last.

"Y'all want another one?" I asked as they sat there with crumbs on their napkins.

"If you don't mind," Kent said, smiling. "You know I can eat about two or three peanut butter and jelly sandwiches myself. I'm a big dude."

I made them each another sandwich and tossed them each a bottle of Coke.

"Thank you, Marcus. I haven't had dinner since last week," Scottie said. His hair was full of large curls and his vanilla face made me think he might've been mixed with something. He and Kent definitely had different fathers, but they both shared their mother's big brown eyes. Scottie sat at the table, swinging his legs back and forth in the chair, his jeans creeping way above his ankles. I felt sorry for them. "I usually just eat at one of my friends' houses or else go hungry."

"Shut up, Scottie. You know we eat dinner at home," Kent said. "He's just lying, Marcus. We have food at home. It's just that my ma is having a hard time this week. We'll get past it."

"It's cool, man," I said, brushing it off. I didn't want to make him any more embarrassed than he already was. "Let's just get started on these math problems. I got a lot of homework myself."

I turned the cartoons on in the living room for Scottie. He stretched out in the middle of the floor while Kent and I sat at the dining room table and studied math. This time my mind wandered. I thought about the woman who was his mother and wondered what she did for a living with her short skirt that would show everything under the sun if she bent over. What kind of job would allow her to dress like that? I wondered where Kent's father was, or Scottie's father, and wondered why they didn't help their mother take care of them. I quickly understood why it was so important for Kent to make it to the NBA—so that he could rescue his family from poverty.

To see a kid like Kent Carpenter at school or on the basketball court, you would never think that he was the same kid who barely had food to eat at home or lived in a house where the water, lights and gas barely stayed on.

Nobody, in their wildest dreams, would ever have guessed. He'd built a wall and hid behind it.

"Look, man, you not gonna run to school and tell everybody that my lights got shut off and stuff, are you?" he asked.

"Are you gonna pass your algebra test on Friday with a C or better?" I asked him.

"What, you blackmailing me?"

"Hey, I got lights on in my house," I said, smiling.

Kent sighed and shook his head.

"Man, you a trip," he said.

"Well?" I asked.

"Well what?"

"You gonna pass the test or what?" I asked. "C or better, man. And I forget everything I saw or heard at your house today."

He thought for a moment, taking in my comments.

"Yeah, man. I'll pass the stupid test," he said.

"C or better?" I asked.

"Whatever, Carter. Let's just get this over with."

I laughed. And before long, Kent was laughing, too.

CHAPTER 10

Marcus

after Kent and Scottie left, I headed up to my room, dropped my backpack in the middle of the floor and turned on my stereo. Young Jeezy's "Go Getta" was on the radio. I pumped it up a little, but not too loud.

After I flipped the switch on my computer and logged into my e-mail, I slipped my jacket off and pulled my jersey over my head. I had twenty-five new e-mail messages since I last checked. I deleted most of them, because they were advertisements and junk mail. Some of them were from girls at school—girls I didn't even know had my e-mail address. One was from my mother telling me about her new job in Houston. She e-mailed me often, sometimes every day.

She was always sending me jokes or photos. She even had a MySpace page and sent messages to my page all the time.

Her message tonight was short and to the point:

Hi, Baby,
How was school today? Spring break is coming soon.
Think about coming for a visit. Call me this weekend.
Love U...Mom

I didn't respond to her e-mail, but made a mental note to call her later when my minutes were free. After I logged out of my e-mail, my Beyoncé screen saver flashing across the screen, I started my workout routine. Did a few push-ups and pumped some iron. The tap on my door interrupted my groove.

"Marcus," my pop called.

I opened the door and my father stood in the doorway wearing coveralls, his hands covered in oil. He was constantly tinkering with the engine of his pickup truck. It was as if he took it apart every day only to put it right back together again.

"Hey, Pop."

"How was school, son?" he asked, the hair on his face desperately needing to be shaved.

"It was cool."

"Game's on tonight," he said. "I'm gonna get

cleaned up. Why don't you come on down and watch the Heat get they behinds beat?"

"You mean the Cavaliers, don't you, Pop?"

"No, I mean the Heat," he said. "The Cavaliers got this one wrapped up tight."

Ever since that rookie, Lebron James, came onto the NBA scene, Pop thought he was the best thing since Michael Jordan. And he was in front of the television set every time the Cleveland Cavaliers played.

"That boy sho' nuff got game," Pop would say about Lebron. "I love to see him play."

He was mesmerized and never missed a game if he could help it.

"Okay, Pop. Let me finish working out and I'll be down in a minute," I said.

"Hurry up," he said and walked toward the bathroom. "I wouldn't want you to miss your boy Shaq getting his behind spanked."

"Whatever, Pop." I laughed and shut my door.

The NBA was all Pop and I had together. That was our quality time—watching the game. Most of the time, Gloria had him wrapped up in one of her projects or had him out at the mall spending all of his hard-earned cash on new furniture and such. Whenever he wanted to spend time with me, I jumped at the chance. It just so happened that my favorite team—the Miami Heat—was playing tonight. But for the most part, I was grateful just to spend time with Pop.

After I finished my last rep, I heard a tap on my window. Then another. As I raised my blinds, I grinned at the sight of Indigo standing in her bedroom window, her hair a wild mass on top of her head.

"What's up?" I asked her.

"What you mean what's up? When were you going to call me?"

"I was going to call. I had to check my e-mail and work out first." I grinned. "You know my routine, girl."

"I guess I don't fit into your little routine anymore since you tutoring the star of the basketball team and all," she said, placing her hands on her small hips.

"I'm the star of the basketball team. What you talking about?"

"Marcus, shut up." She laughed. "You going to that party on Friday night?"

"Doubt it. Are you?"

"I'm trying to build up the nerve to ask my mama if I can spend the night at Jade's house. I wanna go to that party so bad. Everybody's supposed to be there," she said.

"Not everybody."

"Everybody who's anybody."

"What you gon' wear?" Didn't want her looking too good if I wasn't going to be around.

"My new Apple Bottoms jeans with the matching jacket," she said and then went to her closet to get the outfit, and held it up to the window. "See? What you think?"

"Yeah, that's cute," I said, trying to seem interested, but knowing that the game was about to come on. The tip-off was just minutes away and I didn't want to miss it. But didn't want to seem like I didn't care.

"Guess what?" Indigo said.

"What?"

"Nana's here."

"Nana Summer?" I asked.

Now that caught my attention. I loved Indigo's grandmother, Nana Summer. She was a sweet and cool lady. And she could cook! Her cooking was just as good as my grandmother's Creole cooking, and that's saying a lot.

"Of course, Nana Summer! How many nanas do you think I have?"

"What she doing?" I asked.

"She downstairs about to watch the stupid basketball game. She's in love with Shaq."

"For real?" I said, looking for my hoodie. I found

it and pulled it over my head. I couldn't believe that Nana was a Miami Heat fan like I was. "Ask Nana if it's cool if I come over and watch the game with her."

"No," Indi said.

"Yes," I insisted. Why was she being difficult? "I'm on my way over there."

"My father might not like that, Marcus," she said.

"I'll take my chances," I said and slipped my Air Force Ones onto my feet. "Besides, I'm not really coming to see you. I'm coming to see Nana. So he shouldn't have a problem with that."

"Whatever, Marcus," she said.

"I'll be there in a minute," I said before Indigo slammed her window shut.

Pop would understand if I canceled our quality time together. There was plenty of time for that, but it wasn't very often that Nana Summer breezed her beautiful self through town. I swear, if she was about fifty years younger, Indigo might have some competition.

I rushed down the stairs two at a time. Pop and Gloria were cuddled on the couch, the surround sound from our big-screen television echoing through the house as Shaq tipped the ball to one of his other teammates.

"Where you going, son?" Pop asked. "Thought you were watching the game with us."

I had no intention of watching the game with *us,* as Pop put it. I thought I was watching the game with *him.* I had no idea that Gloria had plans of joining us. She didn't even like sports and besides, I thought it was just going to be the fellas. But I was wrong, and as I watched her snuggle up closer to my father, I was grateful that I'd had a change of plans.

"Going next door. Thought I'd watch the game with Nana Summer. She's in town and I just found out that she's a Miami Heat fan."

"Oh, she probably thinks the Heat's gonna win, too."

"Pop, not *think—know* they're going to win," I said, smiling. "How did you put it? Miami got this one wrapped tight."

"Yeah, whatever, Marcus. Don't stay out too late. School's tomorrow."

"Okay, Pop."

"And don't forget to load the dishes before you go to bed," Gloria added. She smiled that devious little smile of hers. She was always competing with me for my father's attention. Guess she won this time, I thought as I bounced out the door.

I had a date with a beautiful older woman, and couldn't be late.

CHAPTER II

Indigo

nana and Marcus were all caught up in the game and in their own little world. It was as if I wasn't even in the room as they both yelled at the television each time Shaq either made a mistake or dunked the ball. My father had even joined in on the fun for a while. That is, until he had to leave all of a sudden. He didn't even seem to mind that Marcus was there on a school night. He was in such a hurry to get to wherever it was he had to go.

"Where you going, Daddy?" I asked.

"Gotta make a run, baby," he said. "I'll be back in a little bit."

I caught Nana cutting her eyes at him, and wondered what that look was for. What was really going on? I would give anything to understand what was happening with my parents, and to be able to fix it so that we could get our lives back to normal. I wanted my father back, the one who stayed home and watched basketball games on television, and a mother who didn't cry so much, and a nana who visited on happy occasions, not rode a Greyhound bus from Chicago to Atlanta in order to play referee to my parents. What was happening to my family?

As Marcus slapped Nana a high five after Shaq dunked the ball, I wanted to follow my father out the door. Trail him until he got to his destination. But instead, I decided to go upstairs and check on my mother. The door was closed and there was silence on the other side. I lightly tapped on the door.

"Mama," I called.

"Come on in, Indi," she said and I slowly pushed the door open.

Mama was in her nightgown, her back against the headboard of the bed, the remote control in her hand.

"What you doing?" I asked.

"Trying to find something good to watch on this television." She smiled. "What you doing?"

"Nothing," I said, and then climbed into bed beside her.

She pushed my hair out of my face. "What's on your mind, Indi?"

"I'm worried about you and Daddy. Are you getting a divorce?"

She sighed, stared at the television for a moment, then turned to face me.

"You're not a little girl anymore, are you, Indigo?"

"No, ma'am."

"Then I'm not going to sugarcoat this for you." Her eyes were soft as she stared into mine. "Your daddy and me are having problems, baby. Sometimes when men get older, they lose sight of what's really important, like family. And they end up looking for things that really don't mean anything in the end. You understand what I'm saying to you?"

"Are you telling me that Daddy's looking for another woman?"

"I'm saying that your daddy is getting older, and sometimes when people get older, it scares them a little. They tend to go soul-searching, and looking for something they already got at home."

She was talking in circles and still trying to sugarcoat things for me, even though she said she wouldn't. Adults were strange. They wanted you to be grown up, but then they still treated you like a child.

"You still love Daddy?"

"Very much so," Mama said. "And he still loves me, and you. We're just having a hard time right now."

"Are you getting a divorce?"

"I doubt it," Mama said. She didn't say no, which meant that she wasn't completely sure. There was still room for doubt, and that doubt lingered in the air.

I was quiet for a moment as I thought this through. It was a lot for me to handle at one time.

"Is Marcus still here?" she asked, interrupting my thoughts.

"Downstairs watching the game with Nana."

"I like him, Indi." Mama smiled, and surprised me with her words. "He's mannerable and respectful. And he seems to like you a lot."

"Yes, he does."

"You two are taking it slow, right?" she asked, and I read between the lines. She wanted to know if we were having sex yet.

"Yes, we are…taking it slow."

"That's good. No need to rush into something that neither of you are ready for. It's not all it's cracked up to be anyway," she said. "But if you find that you can't wait…"

"We're not doing anything, Mama." I interrupted before she could finish her sentence. Didn't feel comfortable at all discussing this with her. Maybe with Nana, but definitely not with my mother.

"Okay, good." I could literally feel her exhale.

My mother had never been the type to discuss boys and sex with me. She hadn't even prepared me for my menstrual cycle and always avoided subjects like that. It was Nana who usually gave me my life's lessons. It was Nana who explained what it meant to have a period and what I should do about it when it was time. Nana was the one who told me what boys will say and do to get into your pants and how I could avoid being taken advantage of. It was Nana who told me that I would know when the right person came along, and that if I couldn't wait, I should always use good judgment.

"You're in the driver's seat, baby," Nana always said. "And don't let anybody make you feel any different. You don't have to do anything before you're ready. You understand?"

"Yes, ma'am," I always answered.

The truth was, I had found someone that I thought was the right person. And I was ready. The problem was, Marcus wasn't ready. Either that or he didn't find me attractive. He probably noticed that I'd picked up a few pounds, which is why I had to make sure I got them off. Nobody wanted a big girl. Not Marcus or the dance team.

It felt weird for my mother to be having this conversation with me. She was never the type to discuss uncomfortable things. I didn't understand her open-ness, but decided to use it to my advantage.

"Mama, is it okay if I spend the night over at Jade's tomorrow? Daddy said it's okay with him, if it's okay with you," I lied, but just a little. Daddy had told me that I needed to ask my mother, although he had already said he was uncomfortable with it. The chance that he'd told my mother about his discomfort was slim, especially considering that they barely spoke to each other these days. I was banking on that being the case as I awaited her answer.

"I don't know, Indi. Your father told me he didn't feel comfortable about that. And I'm not sure I do either."

I was shocked. Daddy had shared his discomfort.

"Daddy said that?"

"Yes, he did," Mama said. "No matter what hap-pens between your father and I, we still both love you very much and have your best interests at heart, no matter what, Indi."

"But, Mommy…"

"Jade's mama doesn't live there and it's just her and her daddy. I don't know about that setup."

"You know Mr. Ernest, Mama. He's a nice man. He would never let anything happen to me. He wants to take me and Jade to see Tyler Perry's new movie." I laughed. "You know the one—*Daddy's Little Girls*. Remember, we saw the previews for it the other night and you were cracking up at that littlest girl. She was so funny. Remember you said she reminded you of Jade when she was little? It's gonna be so good. And you know Jade is my very best friend in the whole world, and we haven't even had a chance to spend any time together since she moved back here."

"I need to speak with Ernest first."

"Okay," I said.

I was almost there. Just say yes, just say yes, just say yes...

"And I'll take you over there just so I can see what kinda living arrangements they got going on."

"No problem," I said. "But Daddy's already been there and took a look around the other day."

"Well, I'll need to see for myself," she said, raising her eyebrows in a way that let me know that she didn't care one bit about what my daddy thought. "And your room needs to be spotless, Indi, before I let you go anywhere. And I'm not kidding."

"Going to clean it up right now." I bounced from the bed and stood in the doorway of my parents' bedroom. "Thanks, Mama."

"Don't thank me yet. I haven't said yes. There are still conditions, young lady."

"I know. But thanks for not saying no." I left the room before she could say another word. In my mind, the answer was yes, and that's what I was going with for now.

I couldn't wait to get Jade on the phone, let her know that we were home free. Well, *almost* home free. I needed to tell her to clean up their house real good and to make it look warm and welcome. She had to get rid of any evidence that Mr. Ernest was never there, and that she practically lived in their two-bedroom apartment alone. It had to look as if an adult lived there 24-7 and that he took good care of Jade, even though he was a single father. Mama had to feel comfortable leaving me there for a whole weekend and that wasn't going to be easy. We had our work cut out for us, and we had to work fast. Friday was just a day away.

I was so excited about spending the weekend at Jade's that I could barely concentrate. I missed everything that was said in my last two classes. All of it was a blur. I sat there on the edge of my seat, waiting for the last bell to ring so I could dash to my locker and then out the door to see if my mama was waiting at the curb.

She was in her usual spot, the engine rumbling as

smoke crept out of the back tailpipe. I rushed to my mama's car with my pink-and-white Filas making a tapping noise on the pavement. I threw my backpack into the backseat right next to my overnight bag. I had packed it the night before and put it in the car on my way to school. Wanted to be ready to go as soon as Mama picked me up; not a minute to spare. I hopped in the front and snapped my seat belt on.

"How was school today?" Mama asked.

"Usual," I said. "Where's Nana?"

"She's at home frying up some fish and got a big pot of spaghetti cooking." She smiled. "Too bad you're gonna miss it."

"I know. But I think Jade's dad cooked dinner for us. Jade said something about him making hamburgers and French fries," I lied. I wasn't even sure that Jade's dad was home. I prayed that he was, but it was a long shot.

The drive there seemed like the longest drive of my life, as I glanced over at the Publix and then at the Walgreen's, praying that everything worked out once we got to Jade's house. Finally, we pulled into the parking lot of her apartment complex, and Mama found a space in front of Jade's brick building. I hopped out and grabbed my bag off the backseat and threw it across my shoulder. Mama was close behind as I led the way up the wooden stairs and to Jade's door. I knocked.

"Hi," Jade said as she swung the door wide open.

Something smelled like ground beef and grilled onions. An old-school Earth, Wind and Fire tune was playing on the stereo in the living room as Jade invited us in.

"Hello, Jade, it's good to see you," Mama said. "Looks like you grew a few inches taller since I saw you last."

"Yes, ma'am, I did." Jade smiled and hugged my mother around her waist. "I'm gonna be tall like my daddy."

"Speaking of Ernest, where is he?" Mama asked.

Oh, boy. Here it comes, I thought. I glanced at Jade with inquisitive eyes. She glanced back. However, I couldn't read her face and that made me nervous. All I could do was wait for the moment of truth. And here it was.

"Oh, he's in his room. Changing out of his work clothes," Jade said. "He asked me to get the burgers started. But he's gonna finish them and cook us some French fries."

"Can you go get him for me?" Mama asked.

"Yes, ma'am," Jade said and then headed down the hallway.

My heart pounded rapidly as I wondered if Mr. Ernest was really at home or if Jade was trying to play my mother. Surely she knew she wasn't dealing with an amateur here. This was the woman who would spank both of us for misbehaving when we were small, and then tell Jade's mom and she'd end up getting another whipping when her mama got home. This was the same woman who could hear everything; no matter what part of the house she was in, she could hear you plotting, planning and scheming and blow your cover with a quickness. She could smell trouble, even before you tried anything. Yes, she was a pro at this parenting thing. And if this first meeting didn't go well, I would never be able to spend the night over here again.

"Carolyn," Mr. Ernest said. His voice was like music to my ears. "How you doing?"

"Doing just fine, Ernest. How 'bout yourself?"

"Couldn't be better," said Mr. Ernest, dressed in a pair of jeans and a sweatshirt. He gave my mother a hug. "Where's that old fart of a husband of yours?"

"Oh, he's probably at home right about now."

"Tell him to come by sometime and holler at me. Drink a beer, watch the game."

"I'll tell him, Ernest." Mama smiled. "You don't mind if Indi spends the weekend, do you?"

"Of course not. I'm glad that Jade will have some-one else to talk to besides me. I know I must drive her crazy, talking her ear off all the time. Nothing like having her best girlfriend around, you know?"

"I agree."

"Can I get you something to drink, Carolyn? Some-thing to eat?" Mr. Ernest asked.

"No, I can't stay. Gotta get home and get the laun-dry started," Mama said. "Indi, I'm gonna let you stay. And I don't even have to tell you to behave yourself."

"I will, Mama."

"And I'll pick you up on Sunday afternoon."

I was so happy, I wanted to jump and shout. Wanted to run down to the second floor and tell that little Hispanic woman—the one who was always peering out her window every time somebody trampled up the stairs—to get used to seeing my face for at least a couple of days.

"Okay, Mama. Tell Nana to save me some of that spaghetti." I gave my mother a strong hug.

"I will," she said, pulling away, adjusting her worn leather purse on her shoulder and heading toward the door. "Mind your manners, Indi."

I barely answered as Mr. Ernest ushered her out the door and I followed Jade down the hall to her bedroom. We had work to do, outfits to pick out, dance routines to practice. We were going to our first high school party and it was going to be the event of the century.

CHAPTER 12

Jade

WE'D waited as long as we could to make an entrance at the party. Didn't want to get there on time and risk being the first ones there. And didn't want to get there too late, either, and miss all the excitement. No, we had to time it just right and spent the first hour on my balcony, watching to see who showed up and what they were wearing. We could hear the music as it began to echo throughout the entire complex.

"You ready?" I asked, smiling.

"I'm ready," Indigo said, shivering from the cold.

My father had already left for the evening, mentioning something about having dinner with Veronica, the woman from the other night. I couldn't believe he had already found a new girlfriend. I wasn't happy about that at all. I'd planned on getting my parents back together and a new girlfriend made it kind of tricky. It was scary thinking that my father could move on that fast. It wasn't a pleasant thought and I squashed it from my mind before it ruined my night.

Indigo and I had already plastered mascara, eye shadow and lip gloss on our faces, before bouncing down the stairs and across the parking lot to the apartment where the loud music and voices were coming from. The lights were low as we walked into the apartment and pressed our way through the crowd of teenagers. Most people were just standing around, either talking or hugging the wall. It didn't seem like a party, because nobody was dancing.

"Come on, Indi, let's show these folks how to party," I said and immediately started moving my hips to the music. As I did the Walk It Out, an ashy-looking boy, much shorter than me, joined me on the floor. I glanced over at Indigo and she was Walking It Out, too. Only her partner was much better looking than mine. Rick Jefferson, a junior, was looking at her as if he wanted to sop her up with a biscuit—like she was gravy or something. But Indi paid him no mind as she bounced to the music.

Within thirty minutes, the three-bedroom apartment on the ground floor of Building Three was filled to capacity with wall-to-wall high school students and a few folks who looked college age, laughing, dancing and posing up in corners of the room trying to get their macks on. The lights became even lower and the music was hypnotizing. Tortilla chips were crushed into the beige carpet, plastic cups sat abandoned around the room—on the coffee table, on window sills or just turned over on the floor—leaving stains from red punch behind. The living room had been converted into a dance floor, and after Indi and I got it started, it was jam-packed. It was hard to move around because there were so many people on the floor.

Chris Moore, one of the basketball team's starting guards, was the deejay for the evening. He had the crowd jumping as he mixed up the CDs, knowing exactly when to play which song. One minute people were loud and shaking their booties out of control, the next minute he slowed it down and people were grinding in every corner of the room. A few people even disappeared into the back bedrooms, doing God only knows what. I would've been back there, too, had someone asked me.

Just as Chris slowed the music down, Chocolate Boy from Mr. Collins's history class walked through the door wearing a pair of sagging jeans and a long-sleeved Sean John shirt. He had no clue that I'd been waiting all night for him to show up, watching the door every time it opened to see if it was him. After a while, I'd given up. Then he walked in and leaned against the wall, a plastic cup in his hand, the bill of his Yankees cap nearly covering his eyes. I wondered if he saw me from across the room checking him out. He must have because he smiled that beautiful smile of his and then winked. I smiled, too.

As the music bounced off the walls, I decided to move my hips to it. Show him what I had. As Crime Mob's "Rock Yo Hips" began to play, I rocked with it until he finally made his way across the room to join me on the floor. I didn't expect him to move like that, but he had rhythm. He leaned toward me and that's when I caught a whiff of his Jordan cologne. I recognized it because my dad had a bottle of it at home.

"What's up, Miss Morgan?" he asked.

"Nothin'."

"Couldn't wait to see you." He smiled that beautiful smile of his, and then stepped back to get a full body view of me. "You lookin' good, too."

"You lookin' pretty good yourself." I flirted with Chocolate Boy. Couldn't even remember his real name. That is, until I heard somebody else call it.

"Hey, Terrence," said the short, bowlegged girl in a pair of jeans that looked like she'd painted them on.

She smiled at him in a way that said they knew each other pretty well. Or maybe she wanted to get to know him a little better. She hugged him.

"What's up, Chante?" Terrence said, but let her go quickly and continued to dance.

"Can I get the next dance?" Chante asked with a grin on her face that made me want to slap it off.

"Nah." Terrence smiled. "I got my dance partner right here."

Before I knew it, I was wrapped in Terrence's strong arms. A different hug than the one he'd just given Chante. The one he gave her was brotherly. The one he gave me was so much more. It felt so good there and at that moment I actually started blushing. Someone had chosen me.

"Whatever," Chante said, rolling her eyes at me, then kept on stepping.

As the sound of Sammie's "Come With Me" began to fill the room, Chocolate Boy moved in closer and we slow danced, moving to each other's rhythm. I was lost in the tenderness of his touch and almost oblivious to the rest of the room. But not too out of it to see Indigo's boyfriend, Marcus, walk through the door. He had sworn to Indigo that he wasn't at all interested in coming to the party and she must've believed him because she was all wrapped up in Rick

Jefferson's arms when he walked in. Didn't even see him. Rick was whispering sweet nothings in Indigo's ear and she didn't seem to mind hearing whatever it was he was saying.

Marcus's jaw was tight as he walked in with Kent Carpenter and a few other basketball players following close behind. Girls seemed to lose their minds when the basketball team walked in, acting like groupies and such like they were a bunch of celebrities or something. In my opinion, they were just average students like the rest of us—they put their pants on one leg at a time just like everybody else. I didn't understand what the hype was all about. I didn't behave that way for nobody.

I wanted to warn Indigo that Marcus was in the house, and that she should tell Rick to remove his fingertips from massaging the small, tender part of her back, but I couldn't seem to get her attention in time. I would've sent her a smoke signal, but the warmth of Chocolate Boy's arms wrapped around my waist had me in a trance. When I opened my mouth to give my best girlfriend a fair warning, a pair of soft lips suddenly covered mine and I was lost, lost in translation, lost in Terrence's strong arms, lost in the moment.

CHAPTER 13

Marcus

at first I thought I was dreaming when I caught a glance at another dude holding on to my girl like she belonged to him. My blood started boiling—literally—and I saw flashes of red, but only for a moment. I started sweating like a pig in heat and suddenly understood what true jealousy felt like. I hadn't felt anything like this in my life and I knew at that moment what I truly felt for Indigo was real.

"Ain't that your woman over there, Marcus?" Kent asked. "She looking like she Rick's woman, the way he pressed all up against her."

"Man, that wouldn't be my woman," Tyler Braxton chimed in. He was one of those players on the basketball team who rode the bench throughout the entire game, and only got playing time when the team was up by twenty points.

"Wouldn't be mine either," Kent said. "Not wrapped up in another dude's arms like that."

The more they talked, the more the heat in the room seemed to rise. My heart started pounding at a rapid pace as I made my way across the crowded room, pressing past sweaty dancing bodies. People were saying hello to me and I barely acknowledged them—didn't even see their faces. Didn't say hello, just kept moving. Indigo's face was the only face I saw in the crowd—hers and Rick Jefferson's. And his held a stupid grin on it—a grin that I desperately wanted to rearrange on his face. As I approached, I acted on impulse. I grabbed Rick by the throat and before I knew my own strength, had him pinned against the grease-stained wall with a cockroach crawling just inches from his bald head.

The music died suddenly and kids gathered around and started chanting and cheering me on.

"Fight!" somebody yelled.

"Beat his behind, Marcus!" someone behind me said.

"Somebody 'bout to fight!" another person went about the apartment yelling.

"What's wrong with you, Marcus?" Rick asked, fear all over his face.

I thought about the day he slapped my jump shot down in practice and then stepped in my face like he'd done something. Got in a huddle with his boys and laughed about it for hours. *Who's laughing now?* I thought. It gave me great pleasure to know that he wasn't laughing anymore, not now, with my fingers wrapped around his Adam's apple.

"If you ever push up on my girl like that again, I will—"

"Marcus!" Indigo yelled and started tugging on the sleeve of my coat. "We were just dancing."

I stared into Rick's face, angry, contemplating whether or not to put my fist to his nose. I could've done so much damage with just one punch, but punching him wouldn't solve anything. Only cause him to punch back, maybe, and probably cause his boys to jump in. Then I'd be fighting with all of them. Maybe Kent and Tyler would jump in and have my back, but I doubted it. The truth was, we weren't that close, and what did they stand to gain by helping me fight my battle? Nothing. Not to mention this was somebody's house. Somebody's mama and daddy made a rent payment on this place every month. As roach infested as it was, it was still somebody's home. I had to consider that.

"Marcus, we were just dancing, man," Rick said finally.

"Yeah? Well it looked like more than dancing to me."

"Marcus, please," Indigo said, her eyes soft and fear written all over her face.

She grabbed on to my arm. I let go of Rick's neck and pulled away from Indigo's touch. I pushed past the crowd. I needed to get outside and get some fresh air, so I could breathe and calm down.

"Marcus, where you going?" Indigo yelled.

I pulled away as she grabbed on to my coat again.

"Leave me alone," I warned her.

"Talk to me," she pleaded.

"We don't have anything to talk about, Indi. Back off," I said and stepped outside into the brisk night air.

This was the one time I wished I'd driven my Jeep. If so, I'd be halfway home by now. Wasn't really feeling the party in the first place, but I had been tutoring Kent when he talked me into coming.

"Let's just ride by and see what's up," Kent had said. "You can just ride with me, Marcus. I'll bring you back to your car."

"Cool," I'd heard myself saying before I had even thought it through. And before I knew it, I was in the backseat of Kent's souped-up Honda Accord, with loud speakers pumping music into my brain and tinted windows that I could barely see out of.

As I stood outside in the cold, I could hear Huey's "Pop, Lock and Drop It" sounding through the entire apartment complex. The music was back on and people were dancing like nothing had ever happened. Like I hadn't just made a complete fool of myself in front of everybody.

"Marcus, I wasn't doing anything with Rick." Indigo's soft voice interrupted my thoughts. She was shivering from the cold and I wanted to offer her my coat.

"It looked like you were having a pretty good time to me," I said, making sure my eyes stayed focused on the streetlight that beamed above. Didn't want to look at her, and avoided eye contact like the plague.

"That's not what it was," Indigo said.

"Oh really? Then what was it?" My eyes remained steady on that streetlight.

"It was just a dance," she said. "I didn't even know you were coming."

"So that's why Rick was rubbing all up on your booty like that? Because you weren't expecting me to show up?"

"He wasn't rubbing—"

"Yo, Marcus," Kent interrupted Indigo, "you ready to bounce, man?"

"Yeah, man," I said, and made my way toward

Kent's car, never turning to look at Indi. Just stuck my hands deep into the pockets of my coat and listened to the sound of my sneakers hitting the pavement as I made my way through the parking lot.

"I was just dancing." She said it softly, but I still heard her.

"Fine, then go back and dance," I told her and kept walking. Never looked back.

Didn't want her to know that my heart was aching. My ego had been threatened when I saw her with someone else and I hid it with anger. Didn't want her to know that I wanted to hold her and hold on so tight that no other dude would ever look her way again. But I camouflaged it with attitude instead.

Left her standing there, shivering in the cold, hoping she would go inside where it was warm. Wanting to wrap my thick coat around her arms to shield her from the brisk night air. What was this thing I was feeling for Indigo Summer—this thing that made me want to forget she ever existed one minute, and want to hold her tight in the very next minute?

CHAPTER 14

Marcus

ONCE inside of Kent's car, Rich Boy's "Throw Some D's" was pumped up again as if he hadn't already played it three times on the way over. I wondered if Kent had another CD, or at least another track on it. He knew every word and sang right along with Rich Boy, pointing his finger and moving his arms with every note of the version they couldn't play on the radio. Tyler pulled something out of his pocket that appeared to be a cigarette at first, but after I looked closely I realized it was a joint. He snapped his lighter, fired up the joint, took a draw, coughed and then looked over at Kent. Kent shook his head and declined. He glanced in the backseat at me.

"Man, don't look back here. I'm not even with

that," I said. "Couldn't you wait until I got out of the car?"

"I thought you needed something to mellow you out, man," Tyler laughed. "After that little issue with your girl and the way you snapped on Rick."

They both laughed.

"Take a hit, Carter," Tyler said.

"Not with it," I repeated, and let my window down, trying desperately not to get in contact with the smoke.

"Marcus, you a punk." Tyler laughed.

"Leave him alone," Kent said and then accelerated as we drove down Old National Highway.

"Call me what you will," I said, staring out of the window, pissed off because of the altercation I'd just had over Indigo. And now, here I was trapped in the backseat of a car with a drug head and still had at least five miles to go before I reached my car. Wondering if this night could get any worse.

"Oh, snap!" Kent yelled. "Blue lights."

It didn't take me long to realize that the blue lights he was referring to were the ones on the police car that had eased up behind us. Hadn't even seen him coming; he'd swooped up out of nowhere. Tyler sprayed something fruity in the car to camouflage the smell of marijuana. Kent slowed the car down and pulled over to the curb. My heart pounded as the blue lights lit up the entire block. All I could do was pray. It was as if God was playing a bad joke on me, and I wanted to tell him, "Man this ain't funny," as the officer approached the driver's side of the car.

Kent's window screeched as he lowered it slowly.

"Hello, sir. Did I go over the speed limit?" Kent asked.

"Is this your car, young man?" the officer asked.

"Yes, sir, it is."

"I need to see your driver's license, registration and proof of insurance please," the blond-haired officer said, and then flashed his flashlight into Tyler's face and then into the backseat of the car. The light from it almost blinded me. "Did you know you have a taillight out? That's why I stopped you."

Kent reached into his back pocket, pulled out his wallet and handed the officer his license. He reached over the sun visor and handed him his insurance card. Then slowly he reached over into the glove compartment and grabbed a thick envelope which I assumed was his car's registration paperwork.

"My taillight is out? I had no idea," Kent said, and sounded just as phony as a two-headed penny.

"Where you fellas off to?" the officer asked, observing Kent's driver's license.

"On our way home from a party, sir," Kent said in his polite voice—the one his mama must've taught him to use when addressing his elders.

"Was there alcohol at this party?" the officer asked.

"No, sir." Kent was laying it on with the politeness.

"Been smoking?"

"No, sir, I don't smoke. Smoking causes cancer."

"Really?" the officer asked, his face like stone. "I'm not talking about cigarettes, son. I'm talking about drugs."

"Oh, no, sir. I don't do drugs, either."

"That's not marijuana I smell all over your car then?" The officer was not convinced.

My heart was pounding so loudly, I could actually hear it, and could feel it in my throat. My stomach began turning flips, and I started inhaling and then exhaling, just trying to get my breathing under control. Was I having an anxiety attack? It was the same feeling I had the day my mother packed up all of her belongings and moved away—leaving her young son behind to live with his father, to face the world without a mother. All that pain suddenly rushed back to my memory, even though I'd spent months trying to make it go away.

"I don't know what you're smelling, sir." Kent's voice cracked a little and I knew he was shaking in his sneakers just like I was. "But it's definitely not mari-juana."

"Of course not, because you boys don't smoke, right?" the officer asked. "I'll be right back. Don't try anything stupid."

I placed my face in the palms of my hands, my heart pounding as every minute felt like a lifetime. How did I end up here, in the car with an idiot and his friend when I knew better?

"I can't believe this, man! I can't believe I let you talk me into getting into the car with you!"

"Chill, Carter," Kent said. "Everything's going to be just fine."

"Here, throw the rest of this out the window," I heard Tyler say, "in case they frisk me."

"Man, I can't throw a bag of weed out the window. Are you crazy?" Kent said.

"Well, do something with it," Tyler said.

"You do something with it. It's your stash." Kent looked frustrated. "I don't know why you gotta smoke that stuff, man!"

"I'll handle it." Tyler stuffed the small plastic bag into the glove compartment of the car, underneath stacks of papers and the car's user manual. He snapped the compartment shut.

"They don't have no reason to frisk any of us," I

said, trying to convince myself more than him that this was just a routine stop. That he'd just receive a warning for having a taillight out and we'd be on our way soon.

"That's right. They have to have probable cause to search you," Tyler said, as if he was an expert on the matter.

"Yeah, and they need a warrant," Kent said, as if that statement changed everything.

Before we could say another word, two more sets of blue lights approached. The first car swooped in front of Kent's car and the other car pulled up beside us. Each car blocked us in, just in case we had intentions of taking someone on a high-speed chase. Officers approached on both sides of the car. A tall slender one with dark hair opened Tyler's door and a short dumpy one, with a receding hairline opened Kent's. They held the doors open, each inviting Kent and Tyler to step out of the car.

"That means you, too, young man." The officer on Kent's side of the car lifted the seat and peered at me. "You need to step out, too."

I didn't put up a fight as I stepped out of the car.

"I need for the three of you to line up, face the car and place your hands on the backs of your heads."

"Are we being arrested?" Kent asked.

"Not yet," Short-and-Dumpy said sarcastically.

"Why are we being asked to step out of the car then? We didn't do anything wrong," Tyler said. "The man just had a broken taillight. But because we're black, we have to stand on the curb and be humiliated like this."

"You haven't seen humiliation," the officer exclaimed. "Now, I would suggest that you simply do as you're asked, young man."

As the officer who initially stopped us approached, the other two officers began to search Kent's car and my heart began to pound at a rapid pace again. Not at the uneven pace as before, but more like the beating of an African drum. Intense.

"You have anything you wanna tell me before my men find something in your car, young man?" he asked.

Kent was silent.

"I don't see how a routine stop for a taillight gives y'all the right to search this man's car," Tyler announced.

"If that young man says one more word, slap the cuffs on him and take him in," the short, dumpy officer said.

"Man, I haven't done anything to warrant an arrest," Tyler continued and I just shook my head. He was making it bad for all of us.

"That's it," Short-and-Dumpy said. He pulled Tyler's hands behind his back, rushed him to the ground, pulled a pair of silver cuffs from his back pocket and wrapped them around Tyler's wrist.

"I know my rights, man," Tyler yelled.

"Yeah, I do, too. You have a right to remain silent... You have a right to an attorney. If you can't afford an attorney, one will be appointed for you..." Short-and-Dumpy grinned.

The tall, dark-haired officer appeared from the other side of the car, carrying Tyler's little plastic bag filled with a green leafy substance.

"My, my, my—what do we have here?" he asked with a grin on his face, swinging the little plastic bag in the air. "What is it you were saying about your rights, young man?"

The officer who'd cuffed Tyler, stood him up, dirt from the sidewalk smeared across his light brown cheek, his mouth poked out. Short-and-Dumpy placed the bag right in Tyler's face.

"What you got to say now, Mister I-Know-My-Rights?"

"It ain't mine," Tyler said, and Kent shot him a quick, nervous glance.

"Well, who in the world does it belong to?" Short-and-Dumpy asked.

"I don't know, but it ain't mine," Tyler said again.

"What about you?" Tall Dark Hair stared directly into my eyes. He was so close, I could literally smell his breath and it wasn't minty fresh. "Is it yours?"

"No," I simply said.

He stared into my eyes, hoping that his intimidation would cause me to confess to it being my stash, but I stared back and didn't even blink. After a few moments he moved on to Kent.

"Is it yours?" he asked, staring directly into Kent's eyes. "Does it belong to you? This *is* your car, right?"

"It's my car, Officer, but that ain't my stuff," Kent said.

"Oh, maybe one of your two buddies here planted it in your glove compartment. Is that what happened?" Short-and-Dumpy chimed in, as Tall Dark Hair attempted to intimidate Kent.

All the while I was praying that someone would claim the stash, so that I could find my way home, to my warm bed and normal life—a life free from drugs, police officers and this nightmare that I had suddenly found myself trapped in.

CHAPTER 15

Indigo

I lay there on a blown-up air mattress in the middle of the floor in Jade's bedroom, staring at the ceiling and listening to Sammie's "You Should Be My Girl" on the *Quiet Storm* on V-103. Joyce Littel had just finished her spiel about love and relationships and I couldn't help but think about Marcus even more. If I could've replayed the night's events, I would've hit the rewind button and started all over again. I never would've let Rick into my space if I'd known that Marcus would react that way. What was I thinking? And now he wasn't answering his phone.

"Why don't you call him again?" Jade said, crunching on a bowl of Frosted Flakes and almost drowning out Sammie with her crunching.

"He's not answering," I said and sat up in bed. I pulled my Chicago Bulls nightshirt over my knees and rested my chin there. "He hates me."

"He don't hate you, Indi. He's just mad."

"I don't even like Rick. That's what's so messed up."

"But he likes you. I could tell by the way he was all up in your face," Jade said. "You think he cute?"

"He's alright. But I never really thought about it."

"Would you go out with him if you weren't Marcus's girl?"

"I don't know, Jade," I said. "I don't even know if I'm Marcus's girl anymore."

"He'll be alright, Indi. He just needs some time," Jade said. "You sure you don't want a bowl of cereal?"

"I'm sure," I told her and tried to think of something else to talk about besides Marcus. "What's up with you and that boy you were dancing with?"

"Terrence?"

"Is that his name?"

"Yep." She smiled and actually blushed. "But I call him Chocolate Boy."

"Ooh, you like him." I smiled back at my friend who was obviously feelin' this Chocolate Boy. I hadn't seen her like that since she first kissed Darren Taylor at the creek behind my house. That was in the fifth grade.

"He all right."

"Just all right?" I asked.

"Yep, just all right. Plus too many girls be up in his face," she said. "I would have to hurt somebody."

"Looked to me like he was feelin' you, too."

"Did I say I was feelin' him, Indi? He just a stupid boy," she said, slurping down the milk in her bowl and leaving the room.

When I heard the little tune playing on my cell phone—the one that alerts me when I have a text message—I grabbed it and flipped open my phone. Prayed it was a text from Marcus. Maybe he'd had time to think things through and was finally ready to talk. Maybe he'd realized that he had overreacted. I knew he would come around. I frowned as I read the text message: How was the party, girl? My mama wouldn't let me go...Tameka. I had hoped it was a text message from Marcus, but it was only from my friend, Tameka. She was supposed to show up at the party, but her mother had other plans for her.

I sent a text message back to her: It was okay. You didn't miss much.

It was true, although there were several kids there and the music was jumping, the party, in my opinion, was just *okay.* I was having a good time until Marcus showed up, causing a scene. After that, I was ready to go. I was embarrassed beyond measure and then I was angry. After being angry for a while I became extremely sad. And that's where I remained—sad.

Jade came back into the room and bounced onto her bed.

"My daddy's home," she said. "And he brought that woman home with him."

"What woman?"

"His so-called girlfriend. Veronica."

"Your dad has a girlfriend?"

"I can't stand her." She rolled her eyes and propped herself up to face me. "She ain't got nothing on my mama."

"Is she pretty?"

"She's okay," she said.

Suddenly I heard old-school music blasting in the living room, followed by roaring laughter.

"I think my daddy got a girlfriend, too."

"For real? Mr. Summer?"

"He's gone all the time, almost every night. He comes home late and my mama's always crying."

"That's how it all starts. That's what happened right before my daddy moved out. He was always gone, and staying out until two and three o'clock in the morning. Even on weeknights." Her eyes became sad. "I knew it, Indi. I knew something bad was about to happen. I could feel it."

"Really?"

"Yep. My stomach would be in knots every night as I watched the clock. It would turn midnight and he wasn't home, then twelve-thirty, then one o'clock. I would be up every night waiting," she said. "Then the next day I would fall asleep in my classes."

"Did your parents know you were staying up all night?"

"Nope," she said. "Next thing I knew, my daddy was moving out."

"I wonder if my daddy will move out soon," I said.

"I don't know," Jade said, shrugging her shoulders. "But you should prepare yourself for the worst. And decide who you wanna live with."

"I'll probably live with my mama. At least Daddy has Nana and my uncle Keith. My mama doesn't have anyone else but me, so I would have to be there for her."

"That's understandable," Jade said. "But good luck trying to get along with her. Mothers turn into witches when the daddies move out. It's like they're possessed or something. And you can't even have a conversation with them. And they get paranoid, like everybody is against them or something. Nope, me and my mama didn't get along at all. She blamed me for us not getting along, but it wasn't me who changed. It was her."

"Well I couldn't leave my mama and move to another state," I told her. I often thought that Jade was brave for leaving her mother in New Jersey like that.

"I didn't have a choice. She forced me out," Jade said, and then got up and shut the door, leaving it cracked just a little bit. "But I got a plan."

"What kinda plan?"

"I'm getting my parents back together."

"How you gon' do that?"

She sat thoughtfully for a moment.

"The same way I ended up back in Atlanta—by misbehaving. Getting into trouble in school is the number-one way of getting your parents' attention. It forces them to talk to each other, because it's *you* that they have in common. Problems with their kids will always get parents talking to each other, even if it's about bad things."

"You think so?"

"I know so," she said confidently. "I just need to come up with a new plan for getting my parents talking again, and more importantly, getting my mama and Mattie back here in Atlanta with my daddy and me."

"So you think if I get into trouble at school my parents will get closer?"

"It'll at least get their attention, force them to talk."

At that moment, I was in awe of Jade's brilliant idea. I never knew she was that smart before, not until I actually started to consider her strategy. It was certainly worth a try to keep my parents together. They needed me more than either of them knew. It seemed that it was up to me to come up with a course of action. I would work on one, but at the moment, I needed a strategy for winning my boyfriend back. That was the issue that was weighing heavy on my mind as I tried Marcus's phone once again.

"Yo, it's Marcus." His deep voice rang through my phone's receiver. "Leave a message at the beep."

I decided not to leave a message this time. I'd already left three, and what good would leaving a fourth one do anyway? I pressed the end key on my cell phone as I glanced over at Jade, who was polishing her toenails with lime-green nail polish—a color that matched her lime-green fingernails with navy-blue tips.

"Marcus is just being stupid, you know. It's not like you were kissing Rick or nothing."

I was silent. My thoughts were on Marcus as an old Luther tune came on the radio. Luther Vandross, although he was much older and way before my time, had a way of making you feel good. He made you think of a boy and wish you were with him at that moment. He had a way of making you fall in love. There, I said it—the "L" word. Love. Was it love that I felt for Marcus? I wasn't sure, but it was certainly a feeling that I hadn't experienced before. And a feeling that I hadn't quite sorted out yet. And I didn't care if Marcus and I never moved to the next level in our relationship. I just wanted my boyfriend back and for things to be just the way they were before.

My head bounced against the pillow in Jade's little bedroom with the Chris Brown and Sammie posters plastered all over the walls. I thought about our conversation and wondered how much time I had before Daddy moved out. It was only a matter of time.

CHAPTER 16

Marcus

My teeth chattered as I shivered from the cold. My arms wrapped around myself as I tried to shield my body from the draft blowing from the air-conditioning. Air-conditioning in the middle of winter? My clothes had been stripped from me and replaced by a set of sleeveless blue coveralls, similar to the ones Pop wore when he worked on his pickup truck, except his were usually covered in oil. As I sat in the holding cell at the youth detention center, I glanced around the room at the sink in one corner of the room and the toilet in the other, and wondered what I was doing here.

I rested my face in the palms of my hands as I re-thought the events that had landed me here. Wondered what I could've done differently. Wondered which choices I'd made that night that were dumb and just plain stupid. All of them, I thought, from the time I got into the car with Kent and Tyler. Even though Kent didn't smoke, he still allowed Tyler to smoke in his car. That was stupid. I never would've guessed that Tyler was a drug head. He gave no indication of it. He was a basketball player who was physically fit and ate a healthy diet. Besides, I knew all of the drug heads at school—the ones who used and the ones who sold. Everybody knew who they were. I would've never thought that one of the basketball players on the team was a user, too. Made me wonder who else on the team used drugs.

I started wondering all sorts of things at that point. When you have a lot of time on your hands, you tend to let your mind wander. Being as though I didn't know who the drug users were made me wonder other stuff, like how many guys on the team were homosexuals. There were a lot of kids at school claiming to be homosexuals—boys liking other boys and girls liking other girls. Especially the girls. They were out of control with this whole concept of being with each other instead of boys. I wondered if they were just experiencing peer pressure or if they really were having homosexual feelings. All in all, I was just

glad Indigo wasn't that type of girl. She liked boys.
She liked me.

At least I thought she did. That is, until I saw her
on the dance floor with Rick. Something inside of me
snapped when I saw them together. I'd worked too
hard to make this girl mine for some other dude to
come along and take her away. But she did run after
me at the party. She did try to explain, but I wasn't
hearing it. What I saw was what I saw and I'd blocked
my mind from all other explanations. My ego was
shattered, and you don't just pick your ego up off the
floor and glue it back together. It takes time for these
things.

Lots of time on my hands, I thought, as my stomach
growled. I'd been promised a sandwich an hour ago
and hadn't received it. At that moment, I would've
accepted whatever concoction my stepmother Gloria
had prepared for dinner. Her meals didn't seem so bad
when compared with the thought of being confined
with limited choices. I would've given anything to be
at home, in our kitchen, eating some of her tuna-fish
surprise or her chicken-and-dumpling casserole. I
wouldn't even have minded hearing her little nagging
voice telling me to take out the trash or to pick my
backpack up off the kitchen floor.

A tear crept down my cheek and I quickly wiped it

away. But then another crept down, and then another. Before long they were all over my face and I couldn't control them. What was I doing? Men don't cry—not like this. Not like girls. They cry inside, holding it in so the world can't see.

"Toughen up, kid," my pop would tell me. And that's what I would do—toughen up. "Don't be crying like no little sissy."

But now it seemed that this was tougher than me and I was a little sissy because I couldn't control it. I was a great negotiator, but I couldn't negotiate with the police officer who'd arrested me. He didn't know that I had a 4.0 grade point average at school, and that I was an ace in math. He didn't know that I played on the school's basketball team and that I tutored other kids in my spare time. People like me didn't go to youth detention centers for possession of marijuana. People like that went to Yale or Harvard—even Morehouse or Clark University.

But I probably wouldn't see the insides of any of those schools. My life was over, and so was my Master Plan. My Master Plan that I'd implemented when I was in the ninth grade—a plan to maintain a 4.0 grade point average (which I had), serve as class president (which I was working on), tutor kids after school (which I was doing when I got into this mess), and volunteer in my community (which I planned on doing this summer). All of this would work to my benefit when I filled out my application for Yale or Princeton. But what was the point now? The minute they saw that I had a record, they'd deny my application on the spot. My Master Plan was down the toilet.

I'd be forced to take over the family business. That's what Pop wanted me to do instead of going to college anyway. He wanted to teach me the odds and ends of selling and managing real estate, or should I say, a bunch of run-down properties in the metro Atlanta area. Most of my father's properties had tenants in them who were consistently late with their rent, but had the perfect excuses for him each month. He did most of the maintenance himself, running around town fixing toilets and replacing hot water heaters instead of hiring someone to do it. That wasn't my idea of a future. Nope, that's where Pop and I bumped heads. But now it seemed I wouldn't have much of a choice. The family business would probably be my future after all.

When I heard keys turning in the lock on the door, I quickly cleaned up my face. Dried away any trace of tears.

"Hey, Carter, you have a visitor. Your father's here," the youth detention officer said.

A visitor? What did he mean, a visitor? Wasn't my father there to take me home and clear my name of all wrongdoings? Pop knew me better than anybody. He knew this was a mistake.

I stood as he led me into another room. As I entered, Pop sat in a chair in the corner of the room with his elbows resting on his knees. He looked up at me, and I tried to read his face quickly, but couldn't really. He looked distraught, or maybe worried. No, maybe it was disappointment that I was reading. Yes, that's what it was, disappointment. I'd let him down, caused him shame. The shame of having to come to a place like this for a son who was in trouble. This picture is not the one I had imagined for Pop and me. He was supposed to attend my basketball games and my high school graduation, not visit me at some youth detention facility.

I dropped my head, looked at my shoes as I entered the room.

"Lift your head up, boy, so I can see your eyes," Pop said.

I did as my father said. The officer left the room and shut the door behind him.

"Hey, Pop."

"Marcus Frederick Henry Carter." He used every one of my names, and that always spelled trouble, made me nervous, assured me I was in trouble. "You explain to me what happened and don't you leave out one single solitary detail."

"Pop, I was tutoring Kent after school, and he talked me into going to this party. I didn't want to go, but he insisted. And he also insisted that I ride with him and Tyler, another dude from the basketball team. We went to the party and I totally embarrassed myself by getting into an altercation with some dude that was pushing up on Indigo—"

"Indigo? What's she got to do with this?"

"I'm getting to that," I said. "Anyway, the three of us left the party together. Kent was taking me to my car, which I had left parked at the school. It's probably still in the school parking lot right now or maybe they towed it by now, I don't know. But that's another story…"

My father stared at me with a blank look on his face, waiting for me to get to the point.

"And so we're driving down Old National Highway, right?"

"Marcus, get to the point," Pop interrupted.

Didn't he say every detail?

"And the next thing I knew there were blue lights behind us and an officer appeared at Kent's window and said that his taillight was out and I thought he would just give him a ticket and send us on our way. But before I knew it two other police cars swooped up, and they had us lined up on the sidewalk like criminals while they searched the car."

"And?"

"And they found some weed in the glove compartment of Kent's car. And since nobody claimed it, they brought us all down to YDC."

"Marcus, were you smoking marijuana?"

"No, Pop. I don't smoke. You know that."

"Look at me in my eyes, son," he said and I lifted my eyes to him. "Was that your marijuana in the glove compartment of that car?"

"No, sir," I said.

"That's all I needed to hear," he said. "They've appointed you an attorney to represent you on Tuesday, but if things get sticky I have a lawyer friend who I can get in contact with."

"Tuesday?" I asked. "You mean I gotta stay here until Tuesday?"

"Marcus, you can't see the judge until then."

"But, Pop, I didn't do anything!"

"I believe you, son, but there's nothing I can do about it tonight. You have to plead your case before the judge on Tuesday morning. Until then, you have to stay here."

"Pop, I can't do that. I got homework to do, and I got basketball practice in the morning. Not to mention I got school and practice again on Monday. I got a project that's due in my science class, and it can't be late."

"Well, Marcus, I don't know what to tell you. You can't see the judge until Tuesday."

I dropped my head and hid my face in the palms of my hands. How did I end up here? But more importantly, how did I get out of here?

CHAPTER 17

Jade

the sound of the final bell bounced against my ears as I slid inside the doorway of Mr. Collins's classroom. I hung my head as I tiptoed to the back of the class, praying Mr. Collins didn't look up from whatever he was doing at his desk. I slid into my seat, easing my backpack onto the floor oh-so-carefully and quietly. Glanced over at Chocolate Boy who gave me a wide grin and then winked.

"What took you so long?" he mouthed to me.

I smiled crookedly and shrugged my shoulders.

"Miss Morgan. I'm certainly glad you were able to grace us with your presence," Mr. Collins said, heading my way. "Do you have a pass?"

"A pass?" I asked.

"Yes. For being late to my class once again."

"No. I don't, sir," I started. "Mr. Collins, I have gym class before this period, and by the time I get showered and dressed, it takes me a long time just to get from the gym to—"

"Miss Morgan, if you don't have a pass to enter my class late, I'm going to have to ask you to leave."

"Leave and go where?"

"To the office, and either get a pass or explain to them why you can't get to my class on time," he said. "I'm also assigning you a detention. You can serve it this afternoon in my classroom. You should be here by three-forty, not a minute after."

"Are you serious?"

"As a heart attack." Mr. Collins didn't even crack a smile. He was serious.

As I stared at him, I noticed that his skin was a flawless dark brown. His teeth were perfectly white and straight, as if he'd worn braces in his childhood. His childhood—I couldn't even imagine that. Mr. Collins, a child? He couldn't have been, I thought, as I wondered what he looked like without that goofy shirt and tie on. I wondered what he looked like on a Saturday afternoon in a jersey and a pair of jeans. I imagined him in casual clothes with a fresh haircut. He was definitely attractive, in an older dude sort of way. But he needed to lighten up a bit. He was too uptight for his own good.

"So you want me to go to the office?" I asked.

"The sooner the better. I'd like to begin teaching my class," he said.

That sarcasm was beginning to wear on my nerves and get a little old. I stood, grabbed my backpack and threw it over my shoulder. Glanced over at Chocolate Boy who gave me a look of sympathy and a half smile. I smiled back and motioned for him to call me later. Since exchanging phone numbers, not a day had gone by that we didn't text or call each other.

As I made my way to the office, my black suede Pumas slapped against the freshly buffed floors in the hallway. I took my time getting to the office, glancing in each classroom along the way, noticing how bored students looked as they struggled to stay awake. When I reached the office, I opened the door slowly. Two boys sat in the waiting area, awaiting their turn in Mr. Gentry's office. He was the blond-haired principal who roamed the hallways confiscating iPods, MP3 players, cell phones and other items that people's parents had purchased with their hard-earned cash.

"I'll get to you guys in a minute." Mr. Gentry's suit seemed identical to the one that Mike Brady wore on the Brady Bunch reruns. His dark-rimmed glasses made him look as ancient as a dinosaur, and his thick mustache needed to have been trimmed months ago. "May I help you, young lady?"

"Mr. Collins sent me down here," I said and rolled my eyes at the thought of Mr. Collins's ridiculous rule. "Today was my third tardy to his class. He said I need a pass from you."

"Miss Kennedy, can you give this young lady a pass to class, please?"

"Yes, Mr. Gentry," Miss Kennedy said and I stepped up to the counter.

"Come with me, boys." Mr. Gentry summoned the two boys into his office. By the looks of it, they'd been fighting. One of them had a torn shirt, while the other had a bloody lip and a long scratch across his pretty brown face. Somebody's mama was definitely about to receive a phone call.

As they reluctantly made their way into Mr. Gentry's office, I awaited my pass from Miss Kennedy.

At three thirty-eight, I slid inside the door of Mr. Collins's classroom. With two minutes to spare, I took a seat at the first desk near the door.

"Pssst." Someone was trying to get my attention. "Hey, girl."

I looked up and there stood Chocolate Boy.

"What's up?" I smiled.

"Got a detention, huh, Miss Morgan?" He smiled as he imitated Mr. Collins. "Miss Morgan, you need to be in your seat ten minutes before the bell rings. Do you understand me?"

"He gets on my nerves." I rolled my eyes at the thought of Mr. Collins's stupid rule, then glanced at my watch. "And where's he at now? I'm on time, and now he's late."

"Can I drive you home from school?" he asked. "Maybe we can go to Chik-Fil-A or Sonic or something...grab something to eat."

"That would be cool." I blushed.

"Hey, how come you don't have a boyfriend?" Chocolate Boy asked and I wanted to tell him that boys just weren't that interested in me.

Before I could answer his question, Mr. Collins popped up out of nowhere.

"Mr. Jeffries, are you serving a detention for me?" Mr. Collins asked.

"No," Terrence answered.

"Then why are you here?"

"I was just talking to Jade."

"Well, you can't talk to Jade because she's serving a detention," he said, stepping inside the room. "Now, if you'll excuse me."

As Mr. Collins shut the door, Chocolate Boy winked his eye and blew me a kiss. I blushed.

I took it upon myself to pull my algebra book out of my backpack, open it and start on my homework.

"You're late, Mr. Collins," I joked and hoped that he had a sense of humor. "Glad you could grace me with your presence."

I was relieved to discover that he did have a sense of humor. I was even more relieved when he smiled and said, "Very funny, Miss Morgan."

"Why you so uptight all the time, Mr. Collins?" I asked, now a little more relaxed around him.

"Why you always late to my class, Miss Morgan?" he said and sat on the edge of his desk, his knees almost touching the desk where I sat.

"I've told you a million times. I have gym before this period. Mr. Collins, you know how far the gym is from here. It takes me forever to get here, and it's not fair for me to be penalized for that."

"It's not like I can make an exception for you, Miss Morgan."

"Call me Jade, please." I was tired of being called Miss Morgan. It made me feel as if I were my mother.

"Okay, Jade." He smiled and literally lit up the entire room. "How do we rectify this situation?"

"Maybe you could talk to Miss Stamps about

letting me leave gym class a few minutes early so that I can get dressed and get here on time."

"Or you could just move a little faster to get here." He moved closer, pressing his legs against the front of the desk, forcing me to lean back a little. "What are you working on?"

"My algebra homework."

"Put it away. I want you pull out your American history book."

I did as he asked. I tucked my algebra book away and pulled my history book out of my backpack.

"What page?"

"Turn to page one seventeen and go to the board," he said. "I would like for you to list the United States presidents from Abraham Lincoln all the way to George Bush, along with the dates that they served in office."

"Are you serious?" I asked.

"That's the second time today that you've asked me that question, Miss Morg—I mean, Jade," he said. "I'm very serious."

"There's no way I can list all the presidents before my detention is over."

"Try."

I slid out of my chair and made my way to the chalkboard, my American history book in tow. No sooner than I began writing on the board, Mr. Collins was right behind me, his fingertips suddenly massaging my shoulders, his warm breath on my neck.

"So, Jade. Is Mr. Jeffries supposed to be your boyfriend?" he whispered.

"He's just a friend," I said, trembling.

"He seems to like you," he said. "You like him, too?"

"Um, I like him a little…"

"Does he touch you, oh-so-gently, like this?"

Before I could protest, his hands moved from my shoulders to the small of my back and wrapped themselves around my waist.

"What are you doing, Mr. Collins?" I asked nervously. No adult had ever touched me this way, and it made me feel out of sorts.

"Turn slowly and face me, Jade," he whispered.

I was stiff, my body refused to move. I stood paralyzed. After a few moments, I did as he asked, turned slowly to face him, trembling like a leaf, my heart pounding rapidly, my eyes staring at the toes of my sneakers. His pelvis pressed against my stomach, and before I could protest, Mr. Collins pulled my chin up, leaned down, and his lips were against mine. Everything inside of me screamed this was wrong, but I allowed it to happen. Closed my eyes and let it happen.

We both jumped when Ludacris's "Money Maker" began to play on my cell phone. I pulled it out of my pocket, flipped it open and stared at the screen. My father.

Mr. Collins moved away and I pressed the green button on my phone.

"Hi, Daddy," I answered.

"Hey, sweetheart, where are you?"

"At school. I had to stay after school for a detention."

"For what, Jade?" he asked and seemed annoyed.

"For being tardy to class," I told him. "It was my third time."

"Jade—"

"Daddy, I'll talk to you about it when I get home."

"Fine. I was calling to see if you wanted to have dinner with Veronica and me. We're going to Red Lobster. Isn't that one of your favorite places?"

"Yes, one of them, Daddy. But I'm really not that hungry," I lied. "I had a big lunch."

"Jade, are you just saying that because Veronica's going?"

"Daddy, I gotta go—" I avoided his question and then started whispering. "I'm in class right now."

"Fine, Jade," he said, "I'll see you at home later."

"Bye, Dad." I didn't give him a chance to respond. Just hit the end key and shut my phone.

I was paranoid. Felt like he could see me through the phone or could tell that I'd done something wrong. Mr. Collins had stepped out of the room. Probably went to tell someone what I'd done and I'd be receiving my suspension soon. My parents would be notified and they'd be shipping me off to juvenile detention or something. I became nervous, started shaking. I went straight for my backpack. Shut my book and stuffed it inside as my heart pounded.

Mr. Collins walked back in and I avoided eye contact.

"Jade," he called.

"Yes," I said, but never looked up.

He touched my chin and lifted my face to him.

"You must not tell anyone—and I mean *anyone*—about what just happened here." His face was like stone and he didn't crack a smile.

He didn't have to tell me that! I wished I could turn back the hands on that big black-and-white clock that hung on the wall. The second hand on it seemed to be ticking so loudly the sound was drowning out my thoughts. After what had happened, I felt like I'd become a woman all of a sudden, when I really just wanted to be a little girl, run home, crawl into bed and pull the covers over my head. Hide the shame.

"Did you hear me, Jade?" Mr. Collins asked again.

"Yes, I heard you," I mumbled. "Can I go home now?"

"Yes, you can," he said.

I didn't waste any time getting out of there; zipped my coat up to my neck, dashed out the door and hustled down the long hallway. The hallway seemed much longer than it had the last time I'd traveled it.

Things were different now. I was different now. And I wasn't sure I liked it at all.

CHAPTER 18

Indigo

I lifted my bedroom window, aimed a Skittle right at Marcus's bedroom window and threw it. It bounced against it, and I threw another. I had decided to give him some space, let him vent and get over his anger, so I'd stopped calling. But when he hadn't shown up for school, I became worried and concerned. Wondered if he was sick. I wanted to go over and knock on his front door just to find out what was really going on. Even though his Jeep had been parked in the school parking lot all day, I figured it had broken down and he'd left it there because he couldn't get it started. I knew he was absent because I'd stalked his locker all day, hoping for just a quick chance to apologize again. Hoping he'd be able to look me in the eye and say that we were done. But he never showed up at his locker, and completely missed his science class, which was odd because he had a project due. He'd been working on that science project for weeks.

Marcus never missed school. In fact, he'd probably had perfect attendance since kindergarten. Something was definitely wrong and I wanted to find out what it was. I threw another Skittle at Marcus's window, to no avail. He didn't even bother to peek through the blinds. Something in the pit of my stomach became uneasy. Marcus wasn't home.

"What if he's been abducted?" I asked myself, plopping down onto my bed. I stared into space for several minutes, contemplating the thought of Marcus being missing like the people you saw on milk cartons and on the little flyers that were plastered on trees and in the windows of barber shops. I heard about things like that on the news, where kids were missing and their parents never found them, and their bodies turned up in the Chattahoochee River months later. What if Marcus was one of those statistics?

I needed to find out! If I hurried, there was still time to rescue Marcus from whatever or whoever had possession of him. Dressed in my flannel pajamas, the light blue and white striped ones that I only wore in the dead of winter, I pulled myself together. I slipped my big fuzzy slippers onto my feet and pulled my coat on, zipping it and bracing for the cold air. I tiptoed past my parents' bedroom and crept down the stairs. They creaked a little, but not enough to stir anyone in the house. Not even Nana, who was sound asleep in the guest bedroom down the hall.

I carefully opened the front door, the brisk air slapping me in the face. Rushed down the stairs and across the yard to Marcus's front porch. As soon as I stepped up onto the porch, I could hear Marcus's dog, Killer, barking uncontrollably. I hated that dog sometimes. He could be so dramatic. Then other times, he could be so sweet and rub up against you like he really liked you. As I rang the doorbell, I took a peek at my watch and realized it was eleven o'clock, and everyone in the Carter household was probably sound asleep, but I didn't care. I needed to know if Mr. Carter knew that his son had been abducted and if he'd already launched a search party.

Killer barked louder as someone approached and turned on the porch light. An eyeball peeked through the curtain on the door and then I heard the clicks of the dead bolt. Mr. Carter stood in front of me in an old worn-out bathrobe, the belt on it barely holding it together. Besides the five o'clock shadow and the gray hair sprinkled on top of his head and all over his face, he looked just like Marcus—just an older version.

"Indi, what are you doing out at this hour?" he asked, pulling the door open and holding on to Killer's collar.

"Hello, Mr. Carter. I'm sorry to bother you this late, but I'm worried about Marcus."

"Oh." He shook his head. "He didn't call you?"

"Call me?" I was confused.

"Come on inside, Indi." He pulled the door open wider. "Have a seat while I let Killer out back."

I stepped inside and slowly walked over to the floral sofa in the living room. I sat on the edge of it, looking over at the table to my left and noticing a photo of Marcus. He was about three years old, his stomach the size of a watermelon and showing from beneath his shirt. He was giggling and the chocolate from his ice cream cone was all over his face. He was so cute. I smiled, but my moment was interrupted as Mr. Carter came back into the room. He sighed as he plopped down in the chair opposite of the sofa.

"Marcus was arrested on Friday night."

"What?" Now that threw me for a loop! Marcus Carter? Arrested? "What for?"

"Apparently he went to some party with that boy… what's his name…uh, that Carpenter boy with the big forehead. Jackie Carpenter's boy."

"Kent?"

"That's him," he said, and pulled his robe tighter. "They were driving around, got stopped, had dope in the car…"

Did he say dope?

"Did you say dope, Mr. Carter?" I asked. "Marcus was smoking dope?"

"He says that he wasn't. And I believe him," Mr. Carter said.

"I saw Marcus at the party that night. He was pretty upset because he saw me dancing with another boy." I don't know why I was telling Marcus's daddy all of this, but I had to talk to someone. Needed to get it out in the open. "But, Mr. Carter, I wasn't interested in that other boy. He's stupid, and he's not even that cute. And I kept trying and trying to talk to Marcus, but he wouldn't listen. And then he wouldn't answer any of my phone calls…and I wish I could tell him how I feel…and…"

My voice began to crack and before I knew it tears were rolling down my face. Here I was in Marcus's living room at eleven o'clock at night, in my striped pajamas and fuzzy slippers, pouring my heart out to his father and crying like a baby. What was wrong with me?

"Sweetheart, Marcus can be a bit stubborn, but I

know he's crazy about you." Mr. Carter smiled and handed me a Kleenex.

"But you didn't see him give me the cold shoulder. He wouldn't even look at me."

"He was probably hurt. Maybe a little jealous. Angry, too. Guys get like that about their girls. But let me tell you, the place where he is right now, he's got a lot of time on his hands. Nothing but time to think. I'm sure he's thinking about you right now."

"For real?"

"For real," he said. "He even asked me about you when I visited him the other day."

"He did?"

"Yes, he did, Indi," he said. "He asked me if I'd seen you. And I told him no. And he said that he was going to call you. Let you know what was going on. Guess he never got around to it. Or maybe he's just a little embarrassed. Embarrassed about the way he acted, and embarrassed because of where he is."

It made me happy to hear Mr. Carter's take on it and that Marcus asked about me. I sat up a little straighter and got myself together.

"Marcus is not a drug head, Mr. Carter. If there were drugs in that car, he wasn't a part of it."

"I know that. We just have to convince the judge of it when he goes to court in the morning."

"He goes to court tomorrow? You think the judge will let him out of jail?"

"Let's hope," he said.

"Can I go with you, Mr. Carter?" I asked. I wanted to be there for Marcus. Show him that I cared.

"Well, I don't know, Indi. I don't think your parents would approve of it."

"Please, Mr. Carter. I'll ask my daddy if I can go. If he says yeah, can I ride with you?"

"I guess it'll be alright. But only if your parents approve."

"Cool. I'm going to ask them right now." I jumped up from the sofa, headed for the door. I turned and gave Mr. Carter a smile. "What time are we leaving?"

"Indi, if you can go, we'll be leaving at eight o'clock in the morning. You can just meet me out front."

"I'll be there."

Before Mr. Carter could say another word, I was out the door and headed across the yard to my front porch.

"And just where have you been, young lady?" Nana's voice in the darkness of the room startled me as I crept inside. "And in your PJs?"

"Hi, Nana," I whispered, hoping that she was the only one in the house still awake.

"Don't 'hi, Nana' me, young lady. Where have you been?"

I sighed, dropped my shoulders and gave Nana my innocent look that usually melted her heart. "I went looking for Marcus."

"At this hour, Indi?" she asked, looking at her watch. "Do you know what time it is?"

"Yes, ma'am. I know what time it is. I thought something was wrong with Marcus when he didn't show up at school today. Nana, he never misses school. And I knew something was wrong."

"And what was it?"

"He's been arrested."

"Arrested?" Her posture changed. She took her hands off her hips. That caught her attention. "What on earth did that boy get arrested for?"

"He was in the car with a couple of knuckleheads—Kent and Tyler from the basketball team—and they had drugs in the car and…"

"Drugs?" She was stunned. "What kinda drugs?"

"Probably weed, Nana. You know, marijuana."

"I know what weed is, little girl!" she said. "Does Marcus smoke weed?"

"No, ma'am."

"Does he sell it?"

"No, ma'am. He was just at the wrong place, at the

wrong time. And now he has to pay for it," I said. "Nana, I wanna go with Mr. Carter in the morning to the courthouse. He said I could go if it's alright with my parents. I wanna be there for Marcus. Can you talk to them for me?"

"I don't know, Indi." She shook her head. This was all too much for her. All too soon, and probably made her think twice about Marcus. But in my heart of hearts, I knew that he was innocent. Knew that he would never do something so stupid. He cared about his future. All he talked about was his Master Plan. This had Tyler Braxton written all over it, and maybe Kent Carpenter, too. I knew that Tyler was a drug head. I saw him with some other boys after school in the courtyard smoking one time. I pretended not to see them and looked the other way. I wasn't sure if Kent smoked. All I knew about him was that all the girls in school had a crush on him, and that he was dumb as a stump. The cheerleaders did his homework. Everybody knew that.

"Nana, I know Marcus. He didn't do anything wrong."

"They don't take you to the juvenile detention center for nothing, Indi."

"Nana, Marcus is a good kid. He doesn't do drugs. He's one of the smartest people I know, besides you.

He's respectful and cool. And if there were drugs in the car, they weren't his. I promise you."

"Hmmm, you really seem to have a lot of trust in this boy. You believe in him, huh?"

"Yes, I do. Nana, you know Marcus, too. You played dominoes with him in the kitchen and watched the basketball game with him just the other night."

"I sure did." Nana chuckled. "Tell you what, Indi. If Mr. Carter don't have a problem with both of us riding to that courthouse in the morning, I'll go with you."

"Really, Nana?"

"Really," she said. "Now get on upstairs to bed. And don't let me catch you running the streets again in your PJs, hair flying in every direction..."

"Thank you, Nana." I kissed my grandmother's plump cheek. "I love you."

"Love you, too, baby."

Nana plopped down in my daddy's recliner, propped her feet up, picked up the remote control and turned on the television.

"Hey, you," she called to me, her glasses at the tip of her nose.

"Yes, ma'am?"

"Marcus called for you this afternoon. Said you were dancing real close with some other nappy-headed boy at that party the other night. Made him real jealous."

"He told you about that?" I was shocked.

"Said that he had no intention of ever speaking to you again..."

"He said that?" That hurt my feelings. It felt as if someone had punched me in my stomach when Nana told me that Marcus had said those words.

"And I told him that if he cared about you, he shouldn't give up on you so easily. Told him that anything worth havin' was worth fightin' for." She smiled.

"And what did he say to that?" I asked, standing there in my PJs and fuzzy slippers.

"He asked me if I could come to court tomorrow with his father, and asked if I could bring you with me," she said, smiling. "So I went over and asked Mr. Carter if I could catch a ride with him."

"You already knew, Nana?"

"I know lots of things, young lady, and don't you forget it." She laughed. "He'll be happy to see your pretty little face in that courtroom tomorrow."

I was without words. I just rushed to my nana, hugged her neck really tight and stayed there for a while. If she was already going to the courthouse, then she knew all along that Marcus was innocent. She just wanted to see if I knew.

Nana was something else.

CHAPTER 19

Marcus

My knees locked underneath the table as I sat next to my court-appointed attorney. Dressed in my navy-blue coveralls, handcuffs on my wrists, I sighed as the judge flipped through my file. Within a few minutes, my pop walked through the double doors behind me, dressed in slacks and a white dress shirt—a look I rarely saw him in. I thought he was alone, until Nana Summer appeared behind him, and behind her, Indigo followed. She smiled as she entered the courtroom, wearing a pair of jeans that hugged her hips and a tight-fitting shirt with the word GUESS plastered across the chest. She looked so beautiful with her wild hair and a smile that made my heart melt. How could I be so angry at someone so pretty? I missed her.

Missed her laugh, her voice, and missed helping her with her math homework. Wished I could hug her and tell her how glad I was to see her. Unfortunately, that wasn't an option.

The three of them plopped down in seats that looked like church pews behind me as the judge asked me to raise my right hand and swear to tell the truth. I felt embarrassed and degraded when I could barely raise my hand because of the cuffs. Felt as if my dignity as a human being had been stripped from me, all because I had made a bad choice, a choice of not being more selective about the people I hung out with. And even though we weren't exactly friends—Kent, Tyler and I—the bottom line was, I was with them. And in the court's eyes, all of us were guilty.

My attorney and the state's attorney went back and forth over the details of the case. They were bouncing back and forth so quickly, I felt as if I were at a tennis match. Apparently Kent and Tyler had both refused to confess to the drugs being theirs, which left my attorney fighting to prove that it wasn't mine. He argued that since it was in the glove compartment of the car, and I was in the backseat, they had no way of proving it belonged to me. And furthermore, they had no way of proving I smoked it or even knew it was there. They threatened to give me a drug test and I was all for it. I knew I didn't have anything to hide. They even asked my father about my behavior at home. Pop was proud to say that I was a model son, an excellent student, and many other great things about me. Even with all this evidence, the judge still wasn't convinced.

"I'm going to place you on conditions, young man. After hearing the testimonies of the other two boys, I'm not convinced that you're totally innocent. You will be monitored over the next few weeks and when you return to court for trial, we'll make a determination about your innocence or your guilt at that time," he said, not even cracking a smile. "Do you understand me?"

"Yes, sir," I said, and it took everything in me not to tell him what I was really feeling.

"We're going to screen you today, to see if you have drugs in your system. Will you pass that screening, son?"

"Of course I will. I haven't been using drugs," I said.

"Fine, we'll see. And then we'll randomly screen you over the next few weeks," he said. "If we find drugs in your system, it's not going to look good for you."

I wanted to say, "Test me today, tomorrow and next year this time and you won't find a thing in my system."

I just simply nodded my head. Even though I wasn't totally cleared, I was glad to be going home.

An officer escorted me to an area where I could have a drug screening done. I sat on a wooden bench awaiting my turn in the restroom, my wrists still in handcuffs, I sat there replaying the events of the traffic stop in my head. I dropped my head, and just as I lifted it, Tyler was being escorted into the room where I sat. His wrists in handcuffs like mine, the officer ordered him to take a seat on the bench next to me.

"They giving you a pee test, too?" he asked.

"Something like that." I wasn't really up for a conversation with this dude and hoped that he wasn't expecting one.

"Sorry you got caught up in this, Carter," he whispered.

"If you're so sorry, why won't you tell the truth?"

He was silent.

"You're next, Carter," the officer said, handing me a small plastic cup. "After you're done, you can just leave the cup in the little compartment on the wall in the bathroom."

I stepped inside the restroom. It smelled of urine and toilet tissue was scattered about on the floor. I went into one of the stalls, attempted to lock it but the lock on it was broken. So I had to hold the door shut while I did what I had to. When I lifted the plastic cup in the air, I noticed that it didn't have a sticker with my name on it like the ones at the doctor's office. Maybe they'll put one on after I'm done, I told myself, and sealed the top on the cup. I slid it into the compartment like the officer had instructed me, washed my hands. Afterwards, I stepped back into the small room where Tyler nervously sat awaiting his fate. He wouldn't have the same outcome as me. We both knew it.

"You're next, Braxton," the officer said, and Tyler stepped into the restroom to pee in his cup.

The ride back to the juvenile detention center in the back of a police car seemed like the longest ride ever. But I was happy just knowing that once I was there, I would simply be retrieving my clothes and waiting for Pop to pick me up. I wasn't staying. And although this had been the worst experience of my life, it had definitely been a learning experience. I was confident that as soon as my test results came back, I'd be cleared of all charges, and all of this would be a long-forgotten memory. Tyler, on the other hand, might not be so lucky. I felt sorry for him, but just a little.

I thought about Kent, too. Wondered what was going on with his case. It didn't take a rocket scientist to know that his mother couldn't afford an attorney to handle his case. His fate would be left up to the court's appointed attorney, and who knew where his loyalty lay. I felt sorry for him. A lot.

He was in for the ride of his life.

CHAPTER 20

Jade

as Chris Brown's "Say Goodbye" rang in my ear, I pulled the covers over my head and sunk my face deeper into the pillow. My stomach turned flips and my head was pounding. I heard Daddy moving around in his bedroom and then in the kitchen, probably packing a bologna sandwich for lunch. Then I heard his footsteps in the hallway, headed toward my bedroom. I buried my head beneath the covers.

"Jade," he called as he opened my door, but I didn't answer. I wanted to pretend I was sleeping. "Jade, baby, why aren't you up? You're gonna be late for school."

I pulled the covers down, but only far enough for my eyes to focus on him. "Daddy, I don't feel so good."

"What's the matter?" he asked and moved closer. He immediately checked my forehead for a fever. "You don't feel hot."

"It's my stomach," I said quickly. "And my head is killing me. Can I stay home?"

He stared for a moment, contemplating whether or not I was telling the truth.

"You don't look good," he finally agreed, sounding more like he was trying to convince himself. "You need me to stay home with you?"

"No, I'll be fine. I just wanna sleep."

"Okay, baby." He looked concerned, but didn't press the issue. My father rarely missed work, and worked in a very busy office. As much as he needed time off and a serious vacation, I didn't need him sticking around, breathing down my neck all day. "You know how to reach me if you need me, right?"

"Yes, Daddy."

"Okay, I'm going into the office," he said. "Call me if you need me."

He left my room, leaving the door cracked just a little. Then I heard the front door shut and the keys jingling as he locked it. I exhaled and pulled the covers over my head again. This time, tears burned my eyes.

I was home free this time, but I couldn't miss school forever. I had to come up with a plan, because there was no way I was setting foot in Mr. Collins's class-room again. How could I face him, knowing what we did? What we did was wrong. What we did had my stomach in knots since that day. What we did made me ashamed to show my face in public again. Even though we were the only two in the room, I felt as if someone else was watching—lurking in the shadows of the room. What if Mr. Collins told all of his other male teacher friends about it and they were all waiting to get me in their classrooms, too? What if he wanted to take it a step further and do more than kissing?

This was all weighing heavy on my mind. The tears began streaming down my face, and I couldn't control them. Chris Brown continued to woo me on the little clock radio resting on my nightstand, *Good Morning America* was on the television set, and I was slowly easing into a deep sleep.

Ludacris's "Money Maker," the ring tone on my cell phone, shook me out of my sleep. I sat straight up, startled for a moment and then grabbed it. Probably Daddy, I thought, until I looked at the screen. *Indigo.* I pressed the talk button.

"Hello."

"Where you at, girl?" she asked right off the bat.

"At home, Indi. Sick."

"Yeah, right." She laughed. "Sick of what? Sick of school? Yeah, me, too."

"No, for real. I'm sick today."

"Jade, you don't sound sick," she said. "Matter of fact, it sounds like you're watching *Judge Joe Brown*."

I immediately grabbed the remote control and turned the volume on the television down.

"I was sleeping."

"It sounds like you're listening to V-103, too," she said, continuing to laugh as I reached over and turned down my clock radio a bit. "What's up with you, girl? How come you're not at school?"

"Indi, I'm really sick today. How many times do I have to tell you?"

"Well, I have good news. Sheila Robinson from the dance team broke her leg yesterday. Well, that's not good news for her, but it's good for you. She can't dance at the game this Saturday, and Miss Martin is looking for a replacement."

"Seriously?"

"Yep, and she asked me about you today." Her words were music to my ears.

"For real, Indi?"

"For real," she said. "She wants you come to tryouts after school tomorrow."

"Oh, wow, I can't believe this!" I yelled.

"So get yourself better before tomorrow, girl. This is your chance."

"Cool. I'll see you tomorrow." I smiled to myself and hung up on Indi before she could say another word.

I jumped out of bed, opened the blinds in my room and let some sunshine in. I checked myself in the mirror and wiped away any sign of tears. Opportunities like this didn't come very often, so I had to get myself together. I sat on the edge of the bed and started contemplating how I could avoid Mr. Collins's class. Maybe I could go to gym, and afterwards pretend to be sick, then spend that entire period in the nurse's office. After his American history class was over, I could miraculously get well and attend my next class. After school, I'd show up for dance team tryouts and be home free. Yes, that was a good plan. It just needed to be executed.

I sat in the nurse's office, a pink slip crumpled in my hand.

"Miss Morgan, what seems to be the problem?" Mrs. Jacobs asked, placing a thermometer under my tongue, and then checking the numbers on it to see if I had a temperature.

"I don't know. I just started feeling bad in my gym class. My head started hurting a little. I was absent yesterday because I was sick. I guess I wasn't fully recovered before I came back to school today."

"Looks that way," Mrs. Jacobs said. "Your temperature is normal, though. Why don't you lie down for a while and see if you feel better."

That was exactly what I wanted Mrs. Jacobs to say—lie down for a while. All I needed was fifty-five minutes. Just long enough to avoid Mr. Collins's American history class.

"That's a good idea," I said in my sick voice, the same one I'd used on my daddy the day before.

"Would you like for me to call your father?" she asked.

"No, ma'am. I just need about an hour to rest."

"Fine. Lie down then," she said. "You can stay until it's time for your next class."

I did just that. Rested on that roll-away bed with a new, crisp white sheet on it. Wellness and nutrition posters were plastered all over the walls in Mrs. Jacobs's office, and I stared at them for a while before pretending to doze off.

When the bell finally sounded, my eyes popped open.

"Do you think you're okay to go to your next

class, Jade?" Mrs. Jacobs asked. "If not, I'll have to call your father."

"I feel much better now," I said. I swung my legs over the side of the bed, lifted my books from her desk and headed for the door. "Bye, Mrs. Jacobs."

"Goodbye, Jade. I hope you feel better."

I rushed through the hallway, zooming past students chattering at lockers. I waltzed into my algebra class, took my seat and opened my book to the page that we were studying. Pulled out my homework that I'd completed on the bus ride to school that morning. I waited for the tardy bell to sound.

Dance team tryouts were just fifty-five minutes away, I thought as I watched the second hand on the clock slowly make its way around and around. I'd successfully avoided Mr. Collins's class for two days in a row, and I suddenly wondered how I could continue to avoid it. What would I do tomorrow and the day after that? Maybe I could get transferred into another history class with another teacher, *female* this time. It was worth a try, worth discussing with my daddy.

I found it hard to sit still as I listened to Miss Jones ramble on about algebraic functions, stuff I wasn't at all interested in. With just ten minutes left on the clock, I became anxious. I was startled when the intercom system buzzed.

"Miss Jones—" Miss Kennedy's high-pitched Southern voice rang through the speakers. "Can you send Jade Morgan to the office please?"

Did she say *Jade Morgan?* This was not happening. I was ten minutes away from my future on the dance team, and Miss Kennedy was calling my name on the intercom system. What could they possibly want with me in the office?

"Yes, I'll send her," Miss Jones responded. "Jade, please take your books with you since we only have a few minutes left in class."

I stood, my heart pounding as I grabbed my books. What was this about? Was my father there to pick me up or something? Maybe Mrs. Jacobs had called him anyway.

I rushed down the two flights of stairs, my pink-and-white Filas bouncing against the shiny tile floor. Made it to the office, and went straight for the counter where Miss Kennedy sat.

"You called for me?" I asked. "Jade Morgan?"

"Oh, yes, Jade." Miss Kennedy sifted through a stack of pink slips that she held for students and handed me the one with my name on it. "Mr. Collins said that you owe him a detention. And since you were sick yesterday and didn't show up for his class today, you need to serve it this afternoon."

"What? A detention for what?" My attitude kicked in. "I served his detention the other day!"

"Apparently he's assigned you another one. You can run on up to his classroom right after the bell rings. But in the meantime, you can have a seat right over there on that bench," she said, pointing her number two pencil toward the wooden bench where students sat and awaited their punishments. She'd pretty much dismissed me, turned toward another student and started giving him instructions.

I stood there for a moment. I still had questions. But she had moved on, so I took a seat on the bench as she'd instructed.

I was at a crossroad—in between a rock and a hard place. I had a decision to make, and it wasn't going to be an easy one. I could run on up to Mr. Collins's classroom, as Miss Kennedy had put it, and be humiliated again or I could avoid him altogether, rush down to the gymnasium for dance team tryouts and suffer the consequences later. My options were slim, and both held consequences.

As I glanced at the clock on the wall one last time, I knew that a decision needed to be made—and fast.

CHAPTER 21

Indigo

as I stepped into the gymnasium, the music bouncing against the walls, I looked for Jade. When I'd seen her in the hallway before lunch, she was waving her Young Jeezy CD in the air—the one she was planning on doing her dance routine to and said that she'd be here. I assumed she would be the first one in the gym, knocking people over just to get to Miss Martin. But as I searched the crowd, she was nowhere in sight.

Girls were already lined up on the bleachers, awaiting their chances. The music had already begun to play as the first girl took her place on the floor. She looked nervous as she began to shake her booty to the music. Watching her took me back to my own dance team tryouts. I remembered how nervous I was. I'd even tripped over my shoestring at one point, and just knew that I was about to be eliminated. But I wasn't eliminated. Miss Martin had chosen me anyway, in spite of my clumsiness. That seemed so long ago. I had forgotten how intense tryouts could be, but suddenly remembered as I watched this girl give it her best shot. She was good, but not nearly as good a dancer as Jade.

If only I knew where she was, I thought as I scanned every inch of the gym with my eyes.

"What's up, girl?" Marcus grabbed me from behind, wrapped his arms around my waist and brushed kisses against my neck. "Who you lookin' for? Me?"

We'd made up since the night at the party. He was so happy to see Nana and I show up in court with his father that he could barely pay attention to the judge—a judge who handed him an unfair verdict in my opinion. As it stood, the drugs in the car could've been either of theirs, and if Tyler had only fessed up, Marcus and Kent might've been set free. Unfortunately, they were all placed on conditions pending further investigation. Marcus was furious! Called Tyler a punk. Accused him of destroying his future. It took all of us—Mr. Carter, Nana and me—just to calm him down on the drive home. It was no secret that Tyler spelled trouble with a capital T.

"I was looking for Jade," I told Marcus. "She's supposed to be trying out for the dance team, and I don't even see her."

"I just saw Jade on the third floor," he said. "She was headed into Mr. Collins's classroom."

"Really? I wonder what she was doing. She's missing dance team tryouts!"

Marcus shrugged. "I don't know, Indi."

"Well, I'm going to find her," I said and swung the door of the gymnasium open. I turned toward Marcus. "You coming or what?"

"Yeah, I'm coming."

I walked at a fast pace through the hallway, up the stairs and to the third floor. Marcus struggled to keep up. Most of the classes were dark and empty inside, except for the journalism class, where students gathered around a table working on a newspaper project.

"Slow down, girl. Why you moving so fast?" Marcus asked.

"We don't have much time to find her. If she misses her turn, she might not get another chance."

When we reached Mr. Collins's classroom, the light was on, but when I tried twisting the door handle, the door was locked. As I peeked through the glass window, Mr. Collins headed toward the door while Jade stood in a corner. Looked like she was crying.

"Why he got the door locked?" I turned to Marcus and asked, as if he knew.

He just shrugged his shoulders.

Mr. Collins saw me and approached the door, un-locking it. "May I help you?"

"I'm here to see Jade," I said and tried looking past him to get a better glance at her. Tried to make sense of what was going on, see if she was really crying. But I couldn't really see her that well. It was a very strange scene, though.

"She's serving a detention right now," Mr. Collins said and tried blocking my view of the room. I stretched my neck around him anyway, just to get a better look. I was right, Jade *was* crying.

Something was wrong, but I wasn't sure what. And Jade just stood there, stiff as a board. She wouldn't even look my way.

"Can I see her for a minute? I have a message from her father," I lied. Desperate times called for desperate measures. I needed to speak to Jade, see her face, and hear her voice. Needed to know that she was alright.

Mr. Collins sighed. He clearly didn't want me to make contact with Jade. Not at that moment. His body language gave me every indication that he wanted me to go away, far away and never come back. Jade was my best friend, and I knew she was in trouble. I couldn't walk away.

"What's the message?" he asked.

"Huh?" I asked, forgetting my lie just that quickly.

"The message from her father—what is it?"

"He um…he wants her to…um…" I was grasping for straws.

"It's a private matter," Marcus jumped in. "It would be too embarrassing to say out loud. We really need to talk to her."

I was grateful to Marcus for speaking up, because I was totally at a loss for words. Mr. Collins stood there for a moment, thought about what Marcus had said.

"Okay, I guess you can see her for a moment."

He shut the door, walked over to Jade and said something to her. He looked as if he was giving her a lecture or scolding her, because she looked scared. After several minutes Jade appeared in the hallway. Whatever tears I'd seen were completely gone. There wasn't even a sign of them.

"What's up?" she asked. "Something wrong with my father?"

"No, we just told him that so he'd let me see you," I said. "What's up with Mr. Collins? Why is he so weird? And why were you crying?"

"I wasn't crying." She was lying.

I know what I saw, and she was definitely crying.

"Did you forget about dance team tryouts? This is your chance to make the team, and it's like you just blew it off." I couldn't understand how she could be so calm about something so important.

She shrugged her shoulders. "I had a detention to serve."

Making the dance team had been our sole purpose in life, and here was her big chance to be on it—or at least try. But she didn't seem interested all of a sudden, and her attitude was bugging me. I wanted to slap some sense into her, grab her around the neck and drag her down to the gymnasium myself. Something had gotten into her, and I wasn't sure what it was. Jade was different. Had been for the past few days. Reminded me of the time when she first got her period. She became standoffish and strange, just like she was now. It took her two weeks to finally come around. Nana had told me to give her some space, said that she'd eventually come around. And she did. Eventually. But not soon enough, in my opinion. Here she was acting the same way all over again.

If she didn't care about being on the dance team, then why should I? I had a spot on the team. This was her future at risk, not mine.

"Fine," I said. "Go back and serve your detention."

She stood there for a moment, like she wanted to say something. Her mind was moving at a rapid pace, I could tell, but she didn't say anything. Just went back into the classroom and slowly shut the door behind her.

"That girl is strange," Marcus said.

"Something's wrong, Marcus. I don't know what it is, but I can feel it."

"Whatever, Indi. I gotta get to practice," he said and headed toward the boys' gymnasium. "You need a ride home later?"

"You know I do."

"Meet me in the parking lot after practice then," he said, facing me and walking backwards down the hall, tossing a basketball into the air.

"Cool." I stood at Mr. Collins's door, contemplating whether or not I should knock again and demand that he tell me what was wrong with my best friend.

I sighed. Headed back to the dance team tryouts. She had made her choice.

I sat on the passenger's side of Marcus's Jeep as we headed toward the old airport, a place where we went every Friday night when the weather was much warmer, to talk and watch the planes land and take off. It was a place that Marcus's father used to take him when he was a kid and they'd talk about serious things. Now it was a place that Marcus took me; a place away from everything else, where we could re-arrange the stars in the sky and discuss our future.

He pulled into the parking lot, gravel rustling beneath his tires. Left the engine running.

"You wanna get out?" he asked.

"No, Marcus, it's too cold out there."

"I'll keep you warm, Indi," he said. "I just wanna get a better view of the stars."

"Alright," I said as I unfastened my seat belt and jumped out.

I met Marcus in front of the car, where he grabbed my hand. He took his thick jacket off and wrapped it around my shoulders.

"I'm sorry about the other night at the party, Indi. I made a complete fool of myself in front of every-body."

"Yes, you did, man. You were tripping!" I laughed, but only a little. Didn't want to hurt his feelings. "But I was flattered that you made a fool of yourself for me."

"You were flattered?"

"I was flattered because it meant that you really care about me, Marcus. No boy has ever cared about me like that before," I said.

"I thought you were with Rick that night, Indi. Like really *with* him, and it made me crazy jealous."

"You don't have to worry about that, Marcus. I'm really *with* you."

He grabbed me and held me so tight. His cold lips soon found mine.

"Indi, I know you're ready to move to the next level, but the truth is, I don't think either one of us is ready for that. I kinda like this place where we are."

"I know, Marcus."

"Can we just take it slow?" he asked.

"Yeah, I would like that," I said.

"Cool," he said and looked toward the sky. "You think you can find the Big Dipper?"

"Yep, it's right there." I pointed it out.

"Where? I don't see it," he said.

"Right there, Marcus," I said, pointing toward the stars. Before I knew it, his lips touched mine again.

I didn't care if we never moved to the next level. I was happy just being right there with Marcus, out in that field, watching rickety old planes take off and land, and counting the stars.

Suddenly it wasn't so cold outside.

CHAPTER 22

Jade

I slid into the passenger seat of my dad's SUV, pulled my seat belt tight and changed his radio station to V-103.

"Well, hello to you, too, Jade-bug," he said.

"Hi, Daddy," I said, and planted a kiss on his cheek. I dropped my backpack on the floor between my feet.

"How was school?" he asked as he pulled away from the curb in front of the school.

"Okay," I said and slid down in my seat. Wished I were at home, where I could bury my head beneath my covers.

"How did the dance team tryouts go? You think you made the team?"

"I'll know tomorrow," I said, knowing that I'd never made it to dance team tryouts.

Mr. Collins had given me a bogus detention to lure me to his classroom. I wasn't there five minutes before he started probing and pawing my body, this time unbuttoning my jeans and trying to cram his hand down into them. I began to cry and begged him to stop, and before I knew it someone was banging on the door, which happened to be conveniently locked. It was Indigo, checking to see why I wasn't at dance team tryouts. I didn't have the guts to tell her that I wasn't at tryouts because I was being molested by my American history teacher. Not to mention he'd already threatened that if I told anyone, he'd deny everything, and I'd be suspended. He said that no one would believe me, and I would end up looking like a fool. Especially since I allowed him to kiss me in the first place.

It was true. The first time his lips met mine, I didn't pull away. Instead, I allowed the kiss. Therefore, I consented to it. That's what Mr. Collins said. In the eyes of the law, he was innocent, because it was consensual, he'd said. Furthermore, he'd done his research and discovered that the reason I'd transferred from my school in New Jersey to this school in Atlanta was because I'd had problems at my old school. He announced that my mother had sent me away because I was a troubled teen.

It was true. I was troubled and I had been sent away. One thing was for sure: this was a secret that I had to keep.

"What's on your mind, Jade-bug?" Daddy asked.

"Nothing," I lied. "Just tired, Daddy. And not feeling very well."

"You haven't been feeling well a lot lately. Maybe I should make you an appointment." He brushed my hair from my face, caressed my cheek.

"I think I'll be okay, Daddy."

He accepted that and I was glad.

"Jade-bug, I know we haven't spent a lot of time together since you've been here. I've been working late hours and spending a lot of time with Veronica, but I promise from now on it's gonna be me and you. Quality time. Just the two of us."

"Okay, Daddy."

"You wanna go over to that Dave and Buster's place that you like so much, eat some good food and play laser tag?"

"I don't really feel like it today. Can I take a rain check?"

"You're not feeling laser tag? Something's wrong." My dad's smile changed to a frown. "Talk to me, Jade.

What's going on?" He pulled his SUV over into the parking lot of a nearby abandoned gas station. As the car's engine rumbled, he turned to face me. Looked me square in the eyes. "What's up?"

"You're never home, Dad. And I feel like I'm raising myself sometimes." It was true. I felt so alone sometimes in that apartment. As much as I used to want my parents to leave me alone and give me space, I really didn't enjoy it once I got it. Even if they nagged me, at least it was conversation. My dad being gone all the time was something that bothered me, but it wasn't my biggest problem. What was bothering me was Mr. Collins, but I couldn't tell my father that. So I had to tell him something. He wasn't going to be satisfied until I did. "You're always with that Veronica woman. It's like you love her more than me."

"Jade, you know that's not true."

"I don't know, Daddy. You're never around, and we don't spend any time together. Not like we used to."

"Okay, I'm trying to fix that right now. As of today, we're spending more quality time together—you and me."

"And I miss Mama and Mattie. I miss seeing them every day."

"I can't really fix that, Jade. Your mother and

Mattie live in New Jersey. You want me to fly you there for a visit during spring break?" he asked.

"That would be fine," I said. "But can you come too, Daddy? Don't you wanna see Mattie?"

"I would love to see Mattie, but I don't think it would be a good idea for me to fly to New Jersey, Jade. Your mother and I don't do well in the same city. It works best with me here and her there," he said. "Besides, Mattie's coming down for the summer."

"She's coming for the summer?" I wasn't up for that. I'd be stuck babysitting her all the time, while Daddy ran around with Veronica. Mattie would be tagging along with me everywhere I went, and my social life would be over.

"Yes, she's coming for the summer, baby."

"So that means that I'm staying here with you—forever?"

"Do you want to?" he asked.

I shrugged and sighed long and hard. Part of me wanted to move back to Jersey, just to be out of harm's way. I loved Atlanta, loved my new high school. I had my best friend back, and had a new potential love in my life. Chocolate Boy really seemed to like me, too, like a real boyfriend, even though we hadn't made it official. I was even close to being on the dance team. That is, until I screwed up my chances by not showing up for dance team tryouts. But this thing with Mr. Collins had me wanting to give all of that up and run back to my mama to get away. I always thought that my dad could rescue me from anything—keep me safe. But the truth was, he had been too busy to rescue me from anything, and way too occupied to keep me safe.

I wanted to tell my dad about Mr. Collins, wanted to blow his cover wide open, but I couldn't. He wouldn't believe me, considering all the trouble I had caused him and my mother. Daddy would think I was doing it again—causing trouble. I couldn't even tell Indigo. She would tell her parents, and then in turn, they would call my parents. I was trapped in a no-win situation, with absolutely no options.

I stepped into my bedroom, turned on my little clock radio. Plopped down onto my bed. When Ludacris's "Money Maker" rang out, I grabbed my cell phone from my purse. Looked at the screen. It was Chocolate Boy.

I picked up. "Hello."

"Hello, stranger," he said. "Where you been hiding?"

"Been sick for a couple of days."

"I was wondering what happened to you the other

day. I was supposed to give you a ride home from school, and take you for a bite to eat. Mr. Collins said you were long gone. And I hadn't really seen you in a couple of days, and I just wondered if I said or did something wrong."

"No."

"Then what is it? I haven't heard from you and you don't return my calls. I been looking for you in Mr. Collins's class, but you don't show up," he said. "I miss your pretty face."

I blushed.

"Sorry." That's all I could think of to say.

"Mr. Collins even asked me about you. Asked me if I'd seen you, like he was all concerned." Chocolate Boy laughed. "Imagine him, concerned."

His words caused my heart to beat fast. Sort of scared me. Was Mr. Collins stalking me?

I knew I had to do something, and fast. There was no way I could go back into that classroom, and definitely not serve another detention after school. I needed to tell someone, get some advice. I needed to spill my guts. I needed my best friend. Indigo.

"Terrence, I have to go. Got something I need to do."

"Only if you promise to hit me back when you're done."

"I promise."

"I'll be waiting," he said, flirting, and I imagined that beautiful smile creeping across his face at that moment.

I hung up before he could say another word. Dialed Indigo's number. It took her forever to pick up.

"What took you so long?" I asked.

"I was loading the dishwasher," she said. Sounded as if she had an attitude. "What's up?"

"I'm sorry about dance team tryouts, Indi."

"It's cool," she said. "It was your own opportunity that you blew."

"I know. You think Miss Martin will give me another chance?"

"Doubt it," she said.

"I need to talk to you, Indi. About something really important, and extremely confidential."

"I'm listening." She sounded a little more concerned, with a lot less attitude.

"Not over the phone. Can't talk about it over the phone."

"Sounds serious, Jade. What's going on?" she asked.

"I'm going to have my dad bring me over. Can you meet me at the creek in fifteen minutes?"

"Why the creek?" she asked. "This must be serious."

"As a heart attack," I said. "I'll see you soon."

* * *

The creek behind Indigo's house is where the most serious discussions of our lives took place. It's where we became blood sisters, each sticking a safety pin in the tips of our index fingers until we saw blood. It's the place where I had my first kiss, while Indigo stood watch for our parents. It's where we talked about sex and boys and discussed our life's goals and dreams. It's the place where we showed each other our breasts when they first started to grow, comparing them to see who had the biggest ones. It's the place where we talked about uncomfortable things like death, especially after that time when our classmate and friend, Keisha Sims, came up missing. And even though posters of her face were plastered all over metro Atlanta, her parents never found her, even to this day. Yep, the creek was a place for serious discussions.

By the time I got there, Indigo was already standing there, pulling her bubble coat tighter and shivering from the cold.

"This must be some deep stuff if you wanted to meet at the creek in the dead of winter," she said. "It's cold out here, girl."

"It is some deep stuff," I told her and pulled the hood of my coat over my head.

"I know what it is. You lost your virginity, didn't you?" she proclaimed.

I looked sheepish. That was something that had happened months ago—I just hadn't shared it with her. It wasn't something I was proud of, since the boy hadn't bothered to stick around afterward. But suddenly I felt embarrassed for not telling Indi.

"You did, didn't you?"

"Indi, I lost my virginity months ago. When I first moved to Jersey. To a boy who wasn't even worthy of my time. Unfortunately, he was just another Quincy. Just wanted one thing. The only difference between you and me is I gave it up. The next day he was with someone else."

"Why didn't you tell me?"

"Well, you were so far away, and you had a new life. You even had a new friend, Tameka. All you ever talked about was Tameka this, and Tameka that. Me and Tameka went to Southlake Mall today. I'm spending the night at Tameka's house."

"Okay, okay. I had a new friend."

"I felt shut out of your life, Indi, just because I wasn't in Atlanta anymore."

"I'm sorry, Jade. I felt shut out of your life, too. You had a new best friend, too, you know. What was her name, Lauren?"

"Didn't take us long to fall out. Last time I saw her, I was about to beat her up." I thought back to the time in the girls' locker room when I had Lauren by the hair, pressed against a locker. She was begging me to let go, and the only reason I did was because a teacher was coming and I couldn't afford to get suspended at that time.

"The fact remains, you didn't tell me about your first time. And that's not cool."

"I was too embarrassed to tell you, Indi," I said. "It wasn't supposed to be like that. I wish I could take the whole thing back, and wish I'd never done it. But I can't take it back. Once you lose your virginity, you never get it back, you know. You never get that first chance again."

"I know, that's why me and Marcus are taking it slow," Indigo said. "But, Jade, we're best friends. We share everything, no matter what."

"I know, and I'm sorry I didn't tell you."

"Oh, you will," she said and then plopped down on a huge rock, folding her arms across her chest. "Now start talking. I wanna know every detail."

"I promise, I'll tell you. But not right now. That's not why we're at the creek."

"Then why are we here, Jade? I'm freezing my behind off."

"Indi, you know my American history teacher, Mr. Collins...he's, uh..."

"He's a pervert is what he is!" she blurted out. "I know some people who had him for American history last semester. I found out that he likes to feel on young girls."

"You mean you knew that he's been touching me?" I asked.

"I wasn't sure, so I started asking around about him. Especially after you missed dance team tryouts and you were crying in his classroom. But then I thought you were just being weird, like that time when you first got your period," she said. "How long has he been doing this?"

"He's done it a couple of times and, Indi, I begged him to stop, but he wouldn't."

"So that's why he had the door locked, right?"

"Yes. He told me that if I told anybody, they wouldn't believe me. Said that I would be suspended from school, especially since I already had some issues at my school in Jersey."

"He's a liar, Jade. What he's doing is not right, no matter what you did in Jersey. You gotta tell somebody."

"I can't tell anyone, Indi, except you," I said, and when my voice cracked, I knew I was about to lose it. Tears rolled down my cheek.

"If you don't tell someone, he'll just keep touching you." She had a point.

"I don't want that either. I don't know what to do."

Indigo wrapped her arms around me. Made me feel safer than I had in a long time.

"We'll think of something," she said. "Don't worry about it. We'll think of something."

I didn't know what solution we'd come up with, but it sure felt good to know that I wasn't alone anymore.

CHAPTER 23

Marcus

my right leg bounced up and down as Pop and I sat in the waiting area. His attorney friend had scheduled an appointment for us to come in and discuss his strategy for my upcoming trial. His office was nice, with mahogany furniture and plush gray carpet. Several copies of *Newsweek* magazine were scattered about on the coffee table in the waiting area. Didn't he subscribe to *Sports Illustrated* or *Vibe* magazine? Neither of those two magazines was there, so I picked up a *Newsweek* instead and started flipping through its pages.

"Mr. Lawrence can see you now," the woman behind the counter finally announced. "If you'll just go down the hall, his office is the first one on the left."

Pop and I made the journey down the hallway, then lightly tapped on Mr. Lawrence's door before entering.

A dark stocky man dressed in an expensive looking suit came from behind his desk and greeted us.

"Rufus, you old buzzard you," he roared with laughter. "What's been going on, man?"

"Everythang is everythang, Melvin. What's been going on with you?" Pop asked.

"Just trying to make ends meet," Mr. Lawrence said. "This your son?"

"This is Marcus."

"A chip off the old block, huh? How you doing, Marcus? I'm Melvin Lawrence."

I took Mr. Lawrence's hand in a firm handshake that almost removed my arm from its socket.

"Hello, Mr. Lawrence," I said, and immediately pulled my arm free. Took a seat on the other side of his desk.

"Call me Melvin. Me and your daddy go way back. I can't even remember how far back, but it's been a long time. Ain't that right, Rufus?"

"Way back, Mel," Pop said and sat next to me.

"Well, let's get down to the business at hand," Melvin said, making his way back to the black leather chair behind his desk. "I received your test results, Marcus...and they're not good."

"What do you mean they're not good, Mel?" Pop asked the question that was burning the tip of my tongue.

"Well, I'm concerned because the results were positive," he said. "That takes us in a whole different direction with this case."

"What do you mean they were positive?" I asked. "That's not possible."

"Marcus, if we're gonna work together, I'm gonna need for you to be straight up with me," Mel said. "It's clear from your results that you were using. Maybe not that night, but at some point. So please, just be honest with me."

"I am being honest with you." I looked at Melvin Lawrence, waiting for him to burst out laughing because obviously this was a joke.

"Marcus, I can't believe I put my trust in you. You stood there and told me point-blank that you hadn't smoked marijuana that night. Now this—"

"Pop, I haven't smoked marijuana. Not once in my entire life."

"Then why are your test results positive, Marcus? Those tests don't lie." Pop was angry. "You made a complete fool out of me."

"Pop, I don't use drugs. You gotta believe me!"

My father gave me a look that I hadn't seen before.

A look of distrust, which was something that we had never shared between us. My father always believed in me, and I believed in him. We didn't always see eye to eye, but we trusted each other. But the look on his face at that moment told a different story. I looked at Mel, and then my father, and then again at Mel. They were convinced that I was both a drug user and a liar.

I stood, and before I knew it I was walking out the door of that attorney's office and slamming it behind me. I stood outside in the parking lot, thinking about my next move. I wanted to break something, hurt somebody, but didn't know what. I zipped my coat up and took off walking down the busy street. Wasn't sure where I was going, but I knew I didn't want to be there, in that attorney's office, listening to him hand me bogus test results. And watching my father turn his back on me. I needed to think, to find some answers. Something was wrong, but I had no proof.

"Marcus," my father called. "Marcus, you get back here!"

I kept walking. I had never disobeyed my father. When he said do something, I did it. But this time, I disobeyed. If he wasn't going to trust me, then why should I obey him? I walked and walked, my heart pounding at a rapid pace. I veered from the main road and took a back street, just in case Pop came looking for me. I didn't want to be found—not by him, not by Benedict Arnold. A father who said that he believed me simply by looking into my eyes, but then turned his back on me in the end. No, I didn't want to be found by him.

The longer I walked, the darker the sky became, and it seemed that I'd been walking forever. It was at least a five-mile walk to my neighborhood, but I made it there eventually. My father's truck was parked in front of our house when I got there. I wasn't ready to face him, but wasn't sure how to avoid him. As I headed toward the creek behind Indigo's house, I heard a voice in the darkness.

"You finally found your way home, did you?" Nana sat on the porch.

"Oh, hey, Nana. I didn't see you over there." I walked toward the porch where Nana was seated in an old rocker. "What are you doing out here? It's cold."

"Waiting for you. Your daddy told me how you walked out of that lawyer's office. He was worried about you."

"Why's he worried?"

"Because he's your father, that's why. What kind of question is that?"

"He doesn't even believe in me when I was telling

him the truth," I said. "Somebody's trying to railroad me, Nana. The results of my drug test came back positive, when I know for sure that I haven't touched any drugs."

"The truth always comes to light, Marcus. No matter what."

"Well, the truth is a lie this time, Nana."

"What do you intend to do about it?" she asked.

"I don't know yet. I hadn't really thought that far. I've just been so angry with Pop and at the situation altogether, that I hadn't even thought about a solution."

"Well, you can't avoid your father for the rest of your life, Marcus. You have to talk to him."

"I will, Nana. I just can't right now," I said. "I just wish I could hit rewind, and start this thing all over again. I wish someone would just step forward and tell the truth."

"Don't count on it, son. Everybody just seems to be denying, and nobody's stepping up to admit to anything," Nana said. "Why don't you tell the truth?"

"I have told the truth, Nana."

"I mean the whole truth, Marcus. You know who the stash belonged to, right?"

"Nana, I'm not a snitch."

"I can appreciate that, son. But don't you think for

one second that either of those boys has the same loyalty to you. If it was your stash in that car, they would've sold you out long ago. You better believe it." She laughed sarcastically.

"You said yourself that the truth always comes to light. No matter what, right?"

"It certainly does," she said. "I remember when I was about your age—maybe a little older. Anyway, I got my first job at the neighborhood pharmacy as a receptionist. When I got my first paycheck, I grabbed up my girlfriend, Mildred, and we took the bus downtown to go shopping. Oh, I was struttin' around, had a pocketbook full of money that day. And I would ask the ladies at the fragrance counters at Macy's to let me smell their perfumes. I tell you, Marcus, by the time we got done spraying all those different fragrances on us, we smelled like two-dollar prostitutes." Nana laughed so hard. "Well, Mildred went one way and I went the other, and we decided to just meet up at the cash registers later. I was looking for a dress for the church picnic. A red one. You see, Reginald Jones was gonna be at that picnic, and I had found out that red was his favorite color. I found the prettiest red dress on Macy's sales rack, and I headed to the counter. I ran into Mildred on the way there. 'Virginia,' she said. 'Look at all this stuff I got.' She had pockets full of costume jewelry. 'Put that stuff back, Mildred,' I told her. 'You gon' get us both in trouble.' 'Oh, Virginia. Stop being silly. You know you want some of this stuff. They have so much, they won't even miss it.' 'I don't wanna be a part of that, Mildred. I'm going to pay for my dress.' 'I'll meet you out front,' she said, and I stood in line at the cash register.

"I looked at the price tag on that dress. It was going to take every penny of my paycheck, but it was well worth it. As I stood in line, I contemplated putting the dress back and finding a cheaper one. But I couldn't, I loved that dress. I wanted it. It was sure to get Reginald's attention at that picnic. I dug my hand deep down into my coat pocket, in hopes that I had some spare change in there. I didn't find any spare change, but what I found was a pair of silver earrings, with little black things dangling off the bottom of them. How did these get into my pocket? I asked myself, looking around to make sure nobody thought I was stealing. When I reached the cashier, I handed her the earrings. 'I don't want these,' I said.

"She grabbed them, threw them aside, and began ringing up my purchase. I opened my pocketbook and pulled out my wad of cash. It was rolled up and secured with a rubber band. I peeled each bill off and handed it to the woman behind the cash register. She stuffed my dress into a plastic bag, handed me a receipt and sent me on my way.

"Just as I was about to head outside, I looked over to my right and two security officers had Mildred in handcuffs. She must've told them we were together because one of them immediately headed my way. 'Hello, miss, can I see what's in your bag?' he asked, and I handed him my bag and my receipt. He looked inside the bag, saw there was nothing more than my red dress, then he checked my receipt. Shrugged his narrow shoulders and eyed his partner who was trying to contain Mildred. 'No, they're in her pocket!' Mildred yelled. *What on earth is she talking about?* I thought. 'The earrings are in her coat pocket.'

"That officer dug deep down into my coat pocket looking for that pair of silver earrings, with little black things dangling off the bottom of them. Mildred had put them there. When he didn't find them, he told me to go. Mildred was taken to the back of the store."

"What happened to Mildred, Nana? Did she get arrested?" I asked.

"Well, first they called her father, who was the minister of our church, by the way. He was a well-respected man in our community, so they probably just gave her a warning or something."

"Did you ever talk to her again?" I asked.

"She showed up at the church picnic. Tried to hold a conversation with me, but I didn't have anything to say to her. You know, I think that even though she got off without any charges, she got the worst punishment of all. She lost my friendship."

"Yeah, she did get the worst punishment," I told Nana. "And even though she tried to bring you down with her, the truth came to light, huh?"

"It always does, baby. It always does."

CHAPTER 24

Jade

It wasn't that hard to convince my father that I was sick another day. That I wasn't able to attend school because I had the same symptoms as before. The only problem was he now threatened to make me an appointment with our family doctor. As I sat on the edge of my bed, my remote control in hand, flipping through the channels, Montel Williams's shiny bald head appeared on the screen. I stopped surfing, and listened to his show. Ironically he was interviewing a young girl who had been molested by her gymnastics coach. She had dreams of becoming a gymnast, but it turned out that those dreams were shattered because she had fallen prey to an adult that she trusted. He had not only molested this young girl, but seven other girls, too.

My eyes were glued to the set as I ate a bowl of Fruity Pebbles and listened to this girl tell her story. She'd eventually built up the nerve to tell her mother. She was so brave, in my opinion, because I hadn't built up enough nerve to do that yet. I was too afraid to share my story with anyone other than Indigo. And she'd been sworn to secrecy. But what Indigo said about Mr. Collins being a pervert kept ringing in my head. I was shocked to discover that there were other girls at my school who had endured the same awful torture that Mr. Collins dished out—that some other girl out there was feeling the same way that I felt at this very moment.

As I listened intently to Montel tell the audience that it was perfectly natural to be afraid to speak up about things like this, my stomach began turning flips. My head started hurting just like it had for the past week. The young girl on the show had a perfect ending to her story because her sick teacher was arrested and was serving time in jail for molesting eight girls. She encouraged girls like me to step forward. Blow the whistle, she said. She had even started an organization called A.C.H.E., which stood for Abused Children Heard Everywhere. She was proud of that organization because it was her way of making something good come out of something bad.

Before the end of the show, my face was soaking wet. It hurt so bad to be in this place—a place that was dark and lonely, not to mention embarrassing and hurtful. It was confusing, too. There was a roller coaster of emotions that I kept feeling, and couldn't share it with anyone. I thought about Mr. Collins's words: "If you tell anyone, I'll deny every word...no one will believe you...everyone knows that you're a problem child, which is why you transferred here from New Jersey. The first time I kissed you, you enjoyed it, didn't you? You asked for this, Miss Morgan, the way you prance into my classroom after the bell rings, drawing attention to yourself. You wanted me to notice you. So don't even think about telling anyone. You'll regret it, if you do."

Thinking of his smelly breath in my ear and the sound of his voice made me sick to my stomach. I wiped my tears away with the back of my hand, and fell to the floor at the foot of my bed. The only way to make this pain stop would be to tell someone. I had to tell my mother. No matter what problems we had in the past, Mommy would understand. She would help me. What if she didn't believe me, though? What if she thought I was just being fast with this grown man, and allowed him to touch me in places that weren't safe? She always talked to me about what a safe touch was, and what an unsafe touch was, but that was so long ago. That was back when I was a little girl. What about now? Did those same rules apply now that I was a teenager? I had to know. I had to tell her. Maybe I could save some other girl from having to go through this, too.

I pulled my cell phone from my purse. Dialed Mommy's number. With each number I dialed, I thought of hanging up. Thought of pushing the end key until I had all ten numbers on the screen. I just stared at them for a moment, each number bright and staring back at me. I pressed the talk button, and there was no turning back. She'd soon be on the other end and I'd have to tell her the truth.

"Hi, baby, what's up?" She was at work, and I knew she couldn't talk long.

"Hi, Mommy," I said.

"Where are you, Jade? Are you at school?"

"No, ma'am, I stayed home today."

"Are you sick?" she asked.

"Well…" My voice shook and she immediately knew something was wrong.

"What's wrong, Jade? Why are you crying?" Couldn't hide anything from her.

"Mommy, I have to tell you something. It's about one of my teachers at school."

"What is it?" she said, impatiently. "Tell me, Jade. Tell Mommy what's wrong."

When she said that, I felt like that little girl again: the one with two pigtails and two front teeth missing, the one she taught about a good touch and a bad touch. I almost backed down, but it was too late. I was too far in it, and there was no turning back now. The best thing to do would be to just blurt it out, get it out in the open and accept whatever consequences followed.

"My American history teacher, Mr. Collins. He um…Mommy, he's been messing with me."

"What do you mean messing with you?"

Here it comes. I'd be called a liar and a trouble-maker. She sounded skeptical, and I was afraid to continue with my story, but I had to.

"One day after school, he kissed me. And he gives me these bogus detentions, just so he can get me in his classroom and touch me…you know…in my private area, Mommy. I'm so sorry." The tears really began to flow at that time. It was out in the open, but I wanted to grab it and put it back in. But it was too late. There was no turning back.

She was silent for a moment, and my heart pounded. I wanted to know what she was thinking.

"You don't have anything to be sorry about, baby." Her words shocked me. She didn't sound mad at all.

Not at first, and not at me. "Where's your father? Have you told him this?"

"No, ma'am."

"He's so busy running around with that new girl-friend of his, that he couldn't even see that something was going on with his own daughter. I'm coming down there!" She was furious. "I'm gonna march right down to that school and beat the crap out of that Mr. Collins. And then I'm going to find out why nobody else at that school stopped him from doing this!"

Mommy was so angry, and that made me nervous. Made me wonder if I'd messed up by telling her.

"Mommy, I'm scared. Mr. Collins said that nobody would believe me, and that there would be consequences if I told."

"I believe you, baby," my mother said. "And yes, there will be consequences, but not for you. For him. Don't you worry. I'll be there soon, and this will all be over. And don't worry about going back to that school. You won't have to face that pervert again!"

"Thank you." I cried harder than I ever had. I wasn't sure if they were tears of joy or sadness. But there was such a relief that came over me, I couldn't help but feel better than I had all week.

I pulled myself up from the floor and dried my tears. This had to be the beginning of the end.

* * *

My father and I stood at the top of the escalator at Hartsfield–Jackson Airport. After Mommy had blasted him about the whole incident, Daddy was at a loss for words. After he'd gotten past the urge to take his shotgun to my school and shoot Mr. Collins, he started with the third degree.

"Why didn't you tell me this was going on, Jade?"

"Daddy, I was scared. Mr. Collins told me not to tell anyone," I explained. "Besides, Daddy, you're never around. I feel like I'm raising myself because you're not there."

"Well, you do have a point. I haven't been there for you like I should have, Jade-bug. Maybe if I had, none of this would've happened to you. Now your mama's all ticked off, and on her way to Atlanta. When we could've handled this—me and you. But you didn't really give me a chance."

"I'm sorry, Daddy. It was just by instinct that I called Mommy. I didn't know what else to do."

"Well, you did the right thing. I'm glad you told one of us." He sighed. "Now if I can just deal with your mama, I'll be alright."

"It'll be okay, Daddy. Her and Mattie staying with us will be just like old times."

"I don't think so, Jade-bug. I…"

"Oh, there they are!" I spotted my mother and sister immediately as they stepped off the huge escalator. Mommy was holding Mattie's hand tightly because she was known to run off and get lost. I started waving my hands in the air like crazy to get their attention. Mattie spotted me right away and took off running toward Daddy and me.

"Daddy!" she exclaimed.

She jumped into his arms and he kissed both her cheeks.

"How's my baby doing?" he asked her.

"Good, Daddy." She kissed him back. "Hi there, Ugly Jade Head."

I popped her upside her head. "Hi, Stinky Girl. What's up with those afro puffs on your head?"

"Your grandmother is responsible for her afro puffs," Mommy said, and hugged me really tight. "How's my girl?"

"Fine, Mommy. You look very pretty," I said and looked over at Daddy to see if he'd noticed, too. She'd lost some weight, and she really looked attractive in her blue pantsuit. She was even wearing makeup. "Daddy, doesn't Mommy look pretty?"

"She certainly does, Jade," Daddy said and kissed Mommy's cheek. "How are you, Barbara?"

"I'm fine, Ernest."

"Daddy, can we eat at the Varsity?" Mattie asked, interrupting the exchange.

"That would be up to your mother and sister," Daddy said.

"Well I don't want the Varsity," I immediately announced and rolled my eyes at my little sister. "How about Red Lobster or something? Remember how we used to go to Red Lobster on special occasions?"

My parents just gave each other a look.

"Are you up for Red Lobster, Barb?" Daddy asked my mother.

"It's either that or the Varsity, and I'm certainly not up for the Varsity," Mommy said. "Sorry, Mattie."

"Mommy," Mattie whined.

"You're welcome to stay at the apartment, if you want to, Barbara. Or I can check you into a hotel if you prefer," Daddy said, and Mattie and I both awaited our mother's response.

"The apartment is fine. We won't be here but a few days. No need wasting money on a hotel," she said. "Unless your *friend* has a problem with it."

She was referring to Daddy's new girlfriend, Veronica. Who cared what she had a problem with? She would just have to deal with it.

"There's no problem with you staying at the apartment, Barbara." Daddy looked annoyed and avoided that conversation like the plague. "Let's go get your bags."

We stood at the baggage-claim area, waiting for Mommy's and Mattie's bags to turn up on the carousel, and once they did, we were out the door. I sat in the backseat of Daddy's SUV, going back and forth with Mattie, while Mommy and Daddy caught up on old times. I couldn't help but smile as they laughed and really enjoyed each other's company. As we drove down Camp Creek Parkway to Red Lobster, I couldn't help thinking how good it felt for all of us to be together again. I missed my family so much. And even if it only lasted for a little while, I wanted to savor the precious moments.

Like I told Indigo, sometimes it took bad things to pull a family back together again.

CHAPTER 25

Marcus

nana was full of fire and spice as she marched past Melvin Lawrence's secretary and right into his office. She held on to my hand tightly as if I was three years old and we were strolling through the mall or something.

"Nana, you're gonna get us arrested," I whispered, as Melvin's secretary chased us down.

"Excuse me, miss, you can't go in there!" She said it way too late, because Nana had already swung the door to his office open.

"Mr. Lawrence, right?" she asked.

"And who are you?" Melvin asked, frowning and looking up from his desk.

"I'm sorry, Mr. Lawrence. I tried to stop her,"

Melvin's secretary said, trembling a little. "You want me to call security?"

"No, it's okay, Nancy," Melvin said after seeing me.

Nancy stood there for a moment longer, bouncing her eyes between Nana and me, and then Melvin. He gave her a nod that let her know that he was not in any danger. She slowly backed out of the door, and pulled it shut behind her.

"Virginia Summer's my name," Nana said, and held her hand out to Melvin. He took it in a handshake.

"Marcus, what is this about?" he asked me, but kept his eye on Nana.

"I'll tell you what it's about," Nana interjected. "The results of this child's drug test are all wrong. This boy don't use no drugs. Now what I need for you to do is march on down to that juvenile courthouse and get the right test results, or tell them that he needs another test."

"With all due respect, ma'am, Miss Summer, you can't just—how did you put it—*march* on down to the courthouse and get some new test results."

"Why not, if they're wrong?"

"That's not how things work—"

"Well, how do things work, Mr. Lawrence? What do you intend to do about this? You're his attorney.

Don't you believe in giving this young man a fair chance? Or are you just taking his father's money?"

"I'm working on Marcus's case right now," he said and held a brown folder in the air. "Marcus needs to come clean. My strategy is for him to admit to smoking marijuana, but deny that the stash in the glove compartment belonged to him. We'll even argue that he wasn't aware of the stash until the officers found it."

"I can't admit to using drugs, Mr. Lawrence. I didn't use any that night or any other night. There must be some mix-up with the test results, because there's no way mine could've been positive."

Melvin sighed long and hard. He plopped down into his leather chair and placed the palm of his hand over his forehead, a look of stress on his face. "You're telling me that you've never used drugs in your life, son?"

"That's exactly what I'm telling you," I said. "I think the drug tests got mixed up or something. I remember that the little plastic cup didn't even have my name or anything on it. Anything could've happened after it left my hands. I'd be willing to bet money that Tyler Braxton's test got mixed up with mine."

"So you're telling me that Tyler was using drugs that night?"

I looked at Nana before answering Melvin's question. To tell the truth about that would mean I was snitching. She gave me a nod, a green light. Sometimes we had to do what it took to save our own behinds. I doubted that Tyler was somewhere telling someone that his test was mixed up with mine. He probably thought that it was a miracle or something.

"Yes, Tyler was using drugs that night," I said.

"Have a seat, son. Let me make a phone call," he said, and Nana relaxed her stance. She removed her hands from her round hips and took a seat in the chair opposite of mine. I had to laugh. Nana didn't play when she wanted some answers. She did what it took to get them. "Yes, Sarah, this is Attorney Melvin Lawrence. I need to find out the results of a young man's drug test...uh, yes...the name is Tyler Braxton..."

Nana sat there, her arms folded across her chest as we both listened intently to Melvin's conversation. After he explained all of the details to the woman on the other end of the phone, he received the answer to the question that had been burning in my mind for two days—what were the results of Tyler's test?

"Uh, yes, thank you, Sarah." He hung up.

"Well?" I asked, on the edge of my seat.

"You were right, Marcus. Tyler Braxton's drug test was negative."

"I knew it! The tests were switched," I shouted. "What do we do now?"

"We'll have to go over to juvenile court to see if we can get you a new test." He stood up and grabbed his suit jacket from a coat rack. "Do you have time to ride over to the courthouse with me?"

"Yes." I stood. "Coming, Nana?"

"Of course I'm coming. What do you think, I'm gonna stay here with Nancy?" Nana chuckled. "She might have me arrested."

"You must be Marcus's grandmother," Melvin said, as he held the door open for us to exit.

"Darn right!" Nana said. "I'm his Nana Summer, and don't you forget it."

She winked at me. I winked back. Made me love her even more.

CHAPTER 26

Indigo

marcus stood there, still posed, wrists bent, as his jump shot went straight into the basket with a swishing noise. The crowd went crazy as his teammates picked him up and bounced him around the court. They met the coach in the middle of the floor and they all jumped around with joy. The game had been close, and they needed that basket so badly. Marcus's shot landed them ahead by two points just before halftime. As the basketball team exited the floor and headed down to the locker room, Marcus's eyes found mine. I blew him a kiss and he winked. I was so glad I got to see that last play; it made me so proud of him.

I stood in the doorway of the gymnasium, pom-poms in my hands, a shiny blue skirt just touching the top of my thigh. When the music began to play, the dance team pranced into the gym in single file, Monique leading the way. We followed her lead as she carried out the routine that we'd practiced all week. Once in the middle of the floor, we formed two lines and the music shook the walls.

I looked into the stands for my parents. I had finally talked them into coming to check out my routine. I spotted them at center court—Mama, Daddy and, of course, Nana. They sat there proudly watching as I twisted and turned to the music. Even Jade and her family were there, seated next to mine. Jade was hoping for an opportunity to talk to Miss Martin after halftime. I thought it was a long shot, but she insisted that she could convince her that she deserved a chance to make up missing tryouts.

Tameka did her cartwheel in the middle of the floor, Jennifer Taylor followed, then me. Just as Monique went in for hers, she just dropped to the floor and landed flat on her back. Her head hit the wood with a loud thump and the entire gym went silent. She just lay there, motionless, until Miss Martin ran over to check her pulse. Before I knew it, her parents had leapt from the bleachers and were standing over her, panicking. The entire faculty had rushed over, and something inside of me seemed to die. What was wrong with her? My heart pounded as I stood at a distance and observed. The other dance team members just stood there next to me, watching as they tried to revive Monique.

"I knew I shouldn't have let her dance tonight," I heard Miss Martin say. "She's been looking sickly."

That was true. Monique had been looking sickly. She went from being a sort of heavy girl to just skin and bones. She was as small as me, and that was a huge change for someone like Monique. My mind drifted back to the conversation we'd had about weight, and how she'd convinced me that the only way to maintain mine was to eat and then get rid of the waste immediately. She'd been doing the same thing for months.

"She has an eating disorder," I heard Jennifer whisper.

"How do you know that?" Monique's mother had heard the comment, even though it was whispered. She was suddenly in Jennifer's face, confronting her. "How do you know she has an eating disorder?"

Jennifer looked intimidated by the woman who looked like an older version of Monique, but she didn't back down. She continued.

"Because all she talked about was losing weight," Jennifer said.

"And maintaining her weight so she could stay on the dance team," Tameka chimed in.

"You girls knew about this?" Miss Martin asked, and at least four girls mumbled a yes.

How could her mother not have known? The drop in her weight was a drastic and noticeable change, and anyone who saw her on a daily basis recognized it. Miss Martin had even asked her if she was sick at practice last week. Monique had given her some excuse, and then laughed it off.

Someone called for an ambulance, and before long, they were carrying Monique off the floor on a stretcher. I said a silent prayer for her. As the dance team exited the floor, the basketball team returned and took their places again. I rushed down to the locker room to change into my clothes, my heart still pounding as I thought constantly about what happened to Monique. I felt uneasy. That very well could've been me instead of her, I thought. Especially since taking her advice, I'd already dropped seven pounds. I wore big bulky clothes at home, sweats and stuff, and big pajamas. No one had even noticed, or if they did, no one said anything. But it was just a matter of time before they did.

"Can we go by the hospital to see if Monique is okay?" I asked as Daddy drove us home from the game.

Daddy looked at me in the rearview mirror and saw the concern on my face. He never said a word, just turned the car around and headed to Grady Medical Center.

The entire dance team must've been just as concerned, because they were all there in the waiting room. Miss Martin was there, too. She was marching back and forth, pacing the floor as if this was her fault. She blamed herself for allowing Monique to dance at halftime.

"When I noticed there was a problem, I should've called her mama," Miss Martin said to no one in particular. She just sort of said it out loud. "How many of you girls are stressing about your weight, and doing unhealthy things like that to your bodies? How many of you are eating and then sticking your finger down your throats?"

All sorts of alarms went off in my head. Each of us looked around at the others. Nobody wanted to admit to that, especially not in front of our parents.

"I've been stressing about my weight a little," Kristal said. "But I've just changed my eating habits."

"Indigo, I've noticed a drop in your weight lately." Miss Martin zeroed in on me.

She just blurted it out of nowhere. I was caught like

a deer in headlights. My heart pounded as my eyes roamed around the room at everyone awaiting my answer. How could she put me on the spot like that? My parents stared at me, waiting for an answer— needing one. I could lie my way out of this one. Miss Martin didn't know for sure, she was just speculating. And as long as I didn't do it anymore, no one ever had to know.

"She's doing better!" Monique's mother saved the day as she walked into the waiting room. "Monique's awake now. Anyone want to go in and see her?"

We all did and all rushed down the hall to Monique's room. As I left the waiting area, I caught a glimpse of Nana sitting in the corner of the room. She gave me a look that said, "You're not slick, little girl. We're gonna visit this subject again later, so don't even think you're off the hook." She said all of that in one little look. Nana was too smart for her own good.

CHAPTER 27

Marcus

this time, sitting in front of the judge, I wore black slacks, a crisp white shirt and a colorful tie—not the blue coveralls and handcuffs that I wore before. Maybe now he was able to see that I was a decent young man, and not the convict that he assumed I was before. The blue coveralls did nothing for my reputation. It's true what they say about appearances. First appearances are usually lasting ones. He'd even had time to review my report card, and see that I was an honor roll student and had been for several years. Not to mention, I had perfect attendance—until now. My next quest would be to see if I could get those two days of school that I missed excused and erased from my record. Yep, that would be my next project.

Once the judge determined that my test results had been confused with Tyler's, he couldn't help but change his attitude toward me. He discovered that not only was I a model student, but a *drug-free* model student at that. And this nightmare had finally come to an end.

"Marcus, I'm sorry for not trusting you," Pop said on the drive home.

"It's okay, Pop. I probably would've done the same thing."

"I should've given you the benefit of the doubt, son, but I just didn't know what to believe." Pop tuned his radio to the oldies station.

"You don't have to worry about me ever getting caught up. I got my future all planned out."

"You've had it planned out since you were about five years old." Pop chuckled. "I should've known better."

"Yep, gotta carry out that Master Plan, you know."

"I know." He looked over at me and smiled. "You going to stay with your mama for spring break?"

"I'm thinking about it. Might be good to get away," I said. "I heard that Houston is really nice."

"What about Indigo? You think you can be away from her for a week?" Pop smiled.

"Yeah, I can be away from her for a week, no problem." I put on my tough act for Pop. "She's just a girl."

"Is that all she is?" he asked.

I couldn't tell Pop that she was the sun and the moon in my world. Couldn't tell him that I thought about her when I woke up in the morning, all day long, and before I closed my eyes at night. And I surely couldn't tell him that I was starting to feel the L word for her. Nope, he didn't need to know all of that.

"Yep, that's all she is, Pop," I lied. "She's just a girl."

I grabbed my iPod out of my coat pocket, put my earphones on and listened to Chris Brown's "Is This Love?" A song that had Indigo Summer written all over it.

CHAPTER 28

Jade

It was as if things were moving in slow motion as I stood in front of the office, my father to my left, my mother to my right. Mr. Gentry stood a few feet away, talking to one of the teachers. Miss Kennedy broke her neck looking on as they escorted Mr. Collins out of school, his arms behind his back in handcuffs. He stared at me as he passed in the hallway, trying to intimidate me. I tried to break the stare, but he kept catching my eyes with his. He was angry, I could tell. But I didn't care. I had done the right thing. In my heart of hearts, I knew that. My heart beat fast, and I squeezed my father's hand tighter.

As soon as my mother had confronted Mr. Gentry

with the news that Mr. Collins had been inappropriate with me, he was doubtful.

"Mr. Collins is one of my best teachers," he'd said.

"What's that got to do with anything, Mr.— What's your name again?" Mommy asked.

"Mr. Gentry." He stirred in his chair, restlessly. Mommy made him nervous.

"That man's accolades as a teacher don't have jack to do with him molesting my daughter!" Mommy was about to get "Sister Girl" on Mr. Gentry. I almost felt sorry for him as sweat began to pop out on his forehead. He was in the fire, and he was definitely feeling it. "Besides, she ain't the only one he's done this to!"

"You know other girls, Jade?" Mr. Gentry looked me square in the eyes.

"Tell him, Jade!" Mommy encouraged me. "Don't shut down on me now."

"Well...um..." I swallowed hard. "My friend Indigo told me there are other girls."

That's when they called Indigo out of class and had her come to the office. She was asked the names of all the girls who had told her about Mr. Collins. She named each of them, and they were all called to the office. That's when I became nervous again, wondering if they would all leave me out there on a limb—wondering if they would protect Mr. Collins and deny that anything ever happened. If they did, I would be left out in the cold, embarrassed, alone, and worse, having to face Mr. Collins again.

Tears covered my face as I listened to every girl tell my story. Each girl confessed that Mr. Collins had touched them in places that were unsafe. They each told about the detentions that he gave for no reason. And they all talked about how they had been sworn to secrecy—even threatened. I was relieved to know that I wasn't alone, but felt sorry that others had to go through what I did.

As I watched Mr. Collins walk past, that smug look on his face, I was grateful that I never had to be intimidated by him again, and that no other girl would fall prey to his advances—ever again. Justice had definitely been served.

That weekend, we were invited to dinner at the Summers' house. My parents and Indigo's parents had been friends for years—family almost. When I walked into their home, I immediately recognized the smell of Nana's fried chicken. Indi's grandmother was the best cook in the whole world, as far as I was concerned. She didn't need recipes, she'd told me once. She just needed a dash of this and dash of that. One day I would understand what she meant by that, but until then I just enjoyed every chance I got to taste her food.

Daddy, Mr. Summer and Marcus's father sat in the family room, beers in each of their hands, shouting at the television while watching the basketball game. The women—Mommy, Mrs. Summer and Marcus's step-mother, Gloria, sat at the dining room table, discussing things that women discuss when they're together—how things are overpriced, where to get it cheaper, and the last stupid thing that their kids did to embarrass them.

In the kitchen, Nana, Marcus, Indigo and me played a game of Spades. Mattie looked on because she was too little to play. But Nana assured her that she could play before the night was over. She was okay with that.

"So, Indi, were you really sticking your finger down your throat after you eat?" I asked. It was a question that had been burning in my mind since that night Monique's head hit the floor at the basketball game. I had been meaning to pull her aside and ask her in private, but decided to go a different route instead. I wanted to do it in front of the people in her life who cared the most about her. Wanted to corner her, em-barrass her—just to be sure she didn't try something so stupid again. She gave me a cross-eyed look. "Well?"

"Yes, baby, we would all like to know the answer to that question," Nana chimed in.

"No doubt," said Marcus.

Indigo's head bounced around the table at each of us. "I did it a few times."

"But you're not doing that anymore, right?" Marcus asked.

"What were you thinking, Indi?" Nana asked.

"I was thinking that I was gaining too many pounds, and would be kicked off the dance team if I got too fat."

"Have you looked in the mirror lately, Indigo? You're far from fat," I said.

"It doesn't matter. People with eating disorders don't see the same things in the mirror that other people do. They see themselves very different than the rest of the world does," she said.

"Kinda like Monique," I said. "She thought she was fat even after she'd lost twenty pounds."

"She's doing better," Indigo said. "She's even picking her weight back up again."

"That's good," Nana said. "I always thought that having an eating disorder was a white-girl thing. But I see that it doesn't matter what color you are. It affects all of our children."

"It's really a self-esteem issue," Marcus said. "Girls are way too concerned about how they look, anyway. It's not that serious."

"Easy for you to say." Indigo slapped the Big Joker on the table, stealing another book for us. She and I were one team, while Marcus and Nana teamed up.

"It was actually a peer pressure thing for Indigo. If Monique hadn't mentioned that Indi was gaining weight, she would've never thought twice about it. But because Monique mentioned that her spot on the dance team might be threatened, Indi felt she had to do something about it," I added. "Right, Indi?"

"How'd you get to be so smart?" Indigo asked. "What are you, a psychologist now?"

"Nope, just a member of the hottest dance team in metro Atlanta!" I wiggled in my chair, and grinned from ear to ear.

"Miss Martin gave you a second chance?" Indigo asked.

"After I explained to her why I had missed tryouts, she picked me for the team. Said that the little routine I did for her at practice that time had her sold. She already knew that she wanted me, even back then. She said she was disappointed when I didn't show up for tryouts."

"Yes!" Indigo said, and gave me a high five.

There was so much excitement that it was hard for us to focus on the game any longer. It didn't take long for Marcus and Nana to whip us under the table in cards. It felt like old times, as old-school music suddenly blared through the speakers and the conversations in the other rooms got louder. Gatherings at Indigo's house hadn't changed one bit.

Mattie had fallen asleep by the time Daddy's SUV pulled into our apartment complex parking lot. Once inside the apartment, I rushed into my bedroom and blew up the air mattress that I had slept on for the past few nights. Although Daddy had offered to let Mommy sleep in his bed and he sleep on the couch, she declined. Instead Mommy and Mattie had shared my bed, and I slept on an air mattress in the middle of the floor. I was glad that Mattie was sleeping with Mommy tonight because she was a terrible sleeper. She was known for kicking and slapping her arm across your face. The next morning you felt as if you had a fight with somebody in the middle of the night.

I took a long bubble bath, sprayed some of Mommy's Victoria's Secret body spray all over me and put on my flannel pajamas. I turned on the clock radio on my nightstand, tuned it to V-103. Hoped Mommy didn't mind listening to the *Quiet Storm* because that's what I used to woo me to sleep. I settled myself onto the air mattress and pulled the covers up. Mattie rushed into the room and bounced onto the bed, wearing her pajamas with the feet in them.

"You can turn off the light now," she said.

"I'm leaving it on for Mommy," I told her and fluffed my pillow.

"She's not coming," Mattie said.

"What are you talking about, silly? She'll be here in a minute."

"I don't think so." She grinned, a huge gap in her mouth where her front tooth used to be. "She's in there with Daddy."

"In where?"

"In his bedroom."

Was she lying? I had to see this for myself. I jumped up, tiptoed into the hallway. All the lights were off in the apartment, except for the light over the stove in the kitchen and the night-light in the bathroom. I crept down the hallway to my father's bedroom. The door was cracked just a little, so I peeked inside. My father's arm rested around my mother's shoulder as they watched the ten o'clock news together. As I heard the newscaster's voice blaring from the television, I couldn't help but smile.

Like I told Indi, sometimes it took bad things to bring your family back together. Just like her little eating issue had her mama and daddy working things out. Her father had been thinking of moving into his own place, but now he'd had a change of heart.

"You can shut that door all the way, young lady," Mommy said.

"Okay."

Mattie started giggling and took off running down the hallway. I didn't even know she was behind me. I started giggling, too, and pulled my parents' door shut tight. I rushed back to my bedroom. I jumped into my bed before she could get to it and pulled the covers up.

"You got the air mattress tonight, Ugly," I told her and threw a pillow upside her head.

"I don't wanna sleep down there by myself, Jade. Can I sleep with you?"

I looked at her for a moment, thought about her request, and then sighed.

"You promise not to kick me?"

"I promise," she lied.

"And I don't want your elbow in my side or your hand across my face when I wake up in the morning."

"I promise, Jade. I promise." She bounced up and down.

"Come on then," I told her.

She didn't waste another minute before she jumped into bed beside me then pulled the covers up to her chin.

"Jade, you think Mommy and Daddy will get back together again? And we'll move back to Atlanta?"

"I don't know, Mattie. Maybe," I said.

* * *

I was hopeful, but I didn't get my hopes up too high. It seemed that just when you thought everything in your life was going good, for some reason, trouble always followed. So I just decided to take each day as it came—slow and easy.

When my phone signaled that I had a new text message, I picked it up, looked at the screen. Chocolate Boy.

Are you sleeping? his text asked.
No, I'm awake. What's up?
Just thinking about you.
What were you thinking?
You wanna go to a movie this weekend?
I'll ask my parents.
Cool.

For a minute I thought he was gone, but then I heard another beep.

You never answered my question...
What was that?
Why don't you have a boyfriend?
Wasn't looking for one...
You want one?

Truthfully, I'd never had a real boyfriend. So the idea had never really crossed my mind until now. I really liked Chocolate Boy, and he didn't seem to want anything from me. Boys always seemed to have an ulterior motive. And he didn't seem to care about the whole Mr. Collins thing. Everybody at school knew about that. I thought it might make it weird between us, but he was the same boy who sat two rows over in my American history class, and sent me text messages all through the day. He was the boy who carried my books when he walked me to class, and held the door for me when we walked through one. He was the boy who told Chante to get lost, because his attention was all on me.

Are you asking to be my boyfriend?

I wanted to be sure, and not make any assumptions.

Yeah...

I wanted to get up out of bed and dance. Wanted to prance around the room, but Mattie had already started breathing hard, like she was asleep. Didn't want to wake her, so I remained calm. Chocolate Boy was asking me to be his girl. Maybe I should leave him hanging until morning, pretend I'd fallen asleep and didn't get his text.

YES. I typed those three letters into my phone, in all caps and hit the send key.

Cool. That was all he said.

I waited for more, but that was it. No more text messages. I guess it was official. Jade Morgan had a boyfriend. And it was...*cool.*

I reached over and shut off the bedside lamp. Let the *Quiet Storm* rock me to sleep. Couldn't wait to see what tomorrow, a day in the life of Jade Morgan, would bring.